PUPPET
ON A STRING

Book III of The O'Shaughnessy Chronicles

by HAROLD WILLIAM THORPE

LITTLE CREEK PRESS
AND BOOK DESIGN

Mineral Point, Wisconsin USA

Little Creek Press and Book Design
A Division of Kristin Mitchell Design, Inc
Mineral Point, Wisconsin
www.littlecreekpress.com

First Printing September 2018

For more information or to order books:
Harold William Thorpe: e: haroldthorpe@hotmail.com
or online at www.haroldwilliamthorpe.com

Printed in the United States of America

Library of Congress Control Number: 2018956989

ISBN-10: 1-942586-45-0
ISBN-13: 978-1-942586-45-6

PUPPET
ON A STRING

Book III of The O'Shaughnessy Chronicles

by HAROLD WILLIAM THORPE

LITTLE CREEK PRESS®
AND BOOK DESIGN

Mineral Point, Wisconsin USA

Little Creek Press and Book Design
A Division of Kristin Mitchell Design, Inc
Mineral Point, Wisconsin
www.littlecreekpress.com

First Printing September 2018

For more information or to order books:
Harold William Thorpe: e: haroldthorpe@hotmail.com
or online at www.haroldwilliamthorpe.com

Printed in the United States of America

Library of Congress Control Number: 2018956989

ISBN-10: 1-942586-45-0
ISBN-13: 978-1-942586-45-6

*I dedicate this book to my daughter, Lisa, and
my daughter-in-laws, Treva and Jodi.*

↦TABLE OF CONTENTS↤

FOREWORD

The *O'Shaughnessy Chronicles* tell the story of my mother, Laura Annette Fitzsimons; her sisters, Anne and Alice; and her parents, Will and Elizabeth Fitzsimons, as they struggle to survive the first half of the 20th century—a century marked by wars, pandemic influenza, the Roaring Twenties, Prohibition, the stock market crash of 1929, and the Great Depression. At 93 years of age, in her book *From High on the Bluff*, my mother chronicled the effect of these events on her family.

My first two novels in the O'Shaughnessy series, *Giddyap Tin Lizzie* and *Bittersweet Harvest,* expand her account by including fictitious people, interactions, and events that add breadth and depth to her stories. Most of the people, places, and events that Mother wrote about have made their way into my books, generally, though, with fabricated names. Mother is Catherine, Alice is Ruby, and Anne is Sharon in my novels. Personalities and relationships in my stories imitate these real-life characters.

The *O'Shaughnessy Chronicles* is set in Iowa County, Wisconsin. *Giddyap Tin Lizzie* takes place in Mineral Point, *Bittersweet Harvest* in Avoca, and the last book in the four-book series, *Strawberry Summer*, is set in Ridgeway. I call these three villages Ashley Springs, Willow, and Logan Junction in my stories. *Puppet on a String* (whose working title was *Sugar 'n' Spice*) spans these villages and much of Iowa County.

Iowa County is bounded on the north by the Wisconsin River a few miles before it merges with the Mississippi River to the west. The county lies within the Driftless Region, an area unlike the rest of the state. Its landscape is distinguished by meandering streams running through V-shaped valleys and rock outcroppings highlighting hills that have road grades as steep as many mountain highways.

This is the look of Wisconsin before the great continental glaciers flattened the hills and filled the valleys. Because of land forms to the north, these great glaciers split and circled southwest Wisconsin and also parts of Illinois, Iowa, and Minnesota, creating this geographic anomaly.

Like the rest of Wisconsin, Iowa County is populated with a mix of English, Irish, German, Scandinavian, and various other ethnicities, but it is renowned for its Cornish immigrants who arrived there in the early 1800s to fuel a lead and zinc mining boom. The Cornish, Cousin Jacks as they were called, were known as the world's foremost hard-rock miners. A large Italian population arrived in the early 1900s to also work the mines. Many like my Irish ancestors came to farm the county's rich soil.

The short stories in *Puppet on a String* elaborate on family relationships that were introduced in *Giddyap Tin Lizzie* and *Bittersweet Harvest*, interactions that enhance the reader's appreciation of dramatic twists and turns they'll read about in the next O'Shaughnessy book, *Strawberry Summer*.

Catherine breaking away from Ruby's dominance is the theme that runs through *Puppet on a String*.

Ruby, two years older than Catherine, is daring, confident, and imaginative. Catherine is captivated by Ruby's nerve and never-ending ideas for creating mischief, accepting Ruby's dominance over her in exchange for excitement and protection. Catherine knows no other way. Ruby's always been her second self.

Catherine is a romantic at heart. As a teenager, she consumed adventure stories and wished she could have lived during the days of Ivanhoe, Robin Hood, and King Arthur. She dreamed the life of Lady Rowena, Maid Marion, and Guinevere.

A large part of Ruby's attraction is that she leads Catherine through a door to adventure that Catherine doesn't have the courage to enter herself. It is fun, exciting, and sometimes reaps delicious rewards. She admires Ruby's cunning and audacity, but she feels guilty when they rain mayhem on family and friends, in part because she never has to take the blame. Everyone knows that Ruby is the instigator.

Ruby has a kind side that Catherine relies on as well. Ruby manipulates and controls, but she protects Catherine, too, leading Catherine to believe that Ruby knows best.

Catherine knows that her sister holds too much influence over her, but she can't pull away. She doesn't fully understand that she's become a puppet on Ruby's string.

Catherine rebels at times, but not for long. It seems to Catherine that whenever she resists Ruby's urgings, things turn out badly. (In *Giddyap Tin Lizzie*, Catherine refused to play a part in the talent show with Ruby. Although she partly acquiesced, the night turned bad for Catherine. She collapsed on stage and almost died with a burst appendix).

The real-life Ruby and Catherine's bond was the same. My mother summarized her relationship with her sister, Alice. She'd laugh and say, "I should have known better, and I suppose I did, but I just couldn't help myself when Alice insisted, 'It's okay, sis, I know what I'm doing.' And I believed her. I thought she was some kind of god or something, so I always did her bidding."

Mother wrote about her cousin Gusta, "When we were in Avoca, my cousin Augusta Stephens came to live with us for one year and went to school there. She was raised in Texas and thought that Alice and I were the world's dumbest country hicks. She was my mother's brother Charlie's only child by his second wife. After Charlie died prematurely, her mother couldn't control her and wrote my mother and asked if she could stay with us awhile to gain some discipline."

Mother continues in her narrative, "When she visited us, she was only sixteen and had the most beautiful clothes, seventy-five and one-hundred-dollar beaded dresses (very expensive for the early 1920s). Alice and I looked like waifs beside her. Gusta was worldlier than any of us, and the teachers in Avoca said she was real smart. We knew that she thought we were pretty naïve, but we liked her despite our different backgrounds, and I know that she liked us, too."

When in my story, Gusta (I kept her real-life name)—Catherine's vivacious, irreverent, and independent-minded Texas cousin—comes to live with the O'Shaughnessy family, Catherine experiences an extraordinary and exciting new world view. Gusta introduces Catherine to a world of possibilities. Catherine is shaken but intrigued by Gusta's outrageous behavior. She discovers that Gusta's an electrified version of her beloved sister Ruby. She'd say, "Gusta's Ruby in high gear."

I introduced the fictional Gusta in my second O'Shaughnessy book, *Bittersweet Harvest*. She arrived at the O'Shaughnessy's, not in the train's passenger car, but standing atop the coal tender, swinging her lariat and singing "Buffalo gals, won't you come out tonight."

And that was only the beginning of her outrageous exploits during the year she spent with Catherine and her family.

Gusta was beholden to no one.

I knew that Mother was very attractive and popular with the young men during those flapper years of the 1920s. But until I read her manuscript, I didn't know about the one man she loved. She never said the name Carl—not until, at 93 years, she wrote her book, *From High on the Bluff*. Now I know, and I feel sadness when I read her story.

Mother was a first-year country school teacher when she met Carl while walking home from school one day. While Mother was dating Carl, she and Alice had fewer interactions because their new jobs as a country school teacher and a live-in nurse required their separation.

I'll tell you Mother and Carl's love story as she told it to me, but I'll tell it through the eyes of my literary characters, Catherine and Jonathon.

After I learned the details of Mother and Carl's relationship, I was intent on describing Jonathon's courting of Catherine with grandeur and fanfare—even introducing an exotic automobile, Jonathon's beloved Bugatti.

Catherine's attraction to this handsome, sophisticated, and dashing man helps unravel the ties that have bound her to Ruby. Ruby's objections to Catherine dating Jonathon reach a fever pitch when Catherine shows courage and turns on her sister—professing her love for Jonathon and accusing Ruby of being jealous, mean-spirited, and spiteful.

But established bonds don't sever easily. Although Catherine was developing independence and a bit of spunk, does she have the courage to break from Ruby and walk through life with this breathtaking man? Can she do this without Ruby's support? Or do events converge to change their relationships forever?

I take liberties in these short stories by adding to Mother's account, introducing the seed (Catherine finding a bundle of perfumed letters) that haunted Catherine and Jonathon's relationship throughout.

Puppet on a String introduces the strong family bonds and tumultuous events that help prepare readers for what will be the fourth book of the *O'Shaughnessy* series. *Strawberry Summer* depicts the rocky relationship between seventy-five-year-old Catherine and her son, Bill—a story that shows Catherine clinging to fond memories of her sister Ruby until a terrible truth is revealed.

This crucible incident in *Strawberry Summer* was spawned by Mother telling me about a letter she didn't receive, a letter that could have changed the rest of her life.

I'll speculate the impact of Mother's missing letter in my fictionalized description of Catherine and Jonathon's relationship. Could I be right?

Puppet on a String presents three sets of short stories, all coupled to Catherine's past and future: the raucous machinations of Catherine, Ruby, and Sharon; Cousin Gusta's everlasting impact upon the O'Shaughnessy family; and Jonathon's courting Catherine. These people and events are seen through Catherine's eyes, from her point of view.

TIES
THAT
BIND

1

A BAD MAN AT THE CIRCUS

Author's Note
Although it's likely that Mother and her sisters would have attended a circus in their youth, she never mentioned it. I include it here because it contrasts the literal puppet on a string with the symbolic puppet on a string. It also introduces Catherine to her badly maimed but kindly Uncle Jesse, an uncle who plays an important role in her later life.

It still scares me when I think about that day. I never attended a circus again. But I'd been warned. Grandma told me that naughty men worked for the circus. In those days, I didn't even know what a naughty man was. Heavens, the only naughty man I could think of was Uncle Frank, because he frowned all the time. He was no fun at all, but I didn't see him much. I didn't learn until later that I had another uncle, too. I met him that day at the circus, the day I learned that a person could be a puppet on a string.

We were visiting Grandma Tregonning in Hinton, and she had given us each a quarter to spend. As we left Grandma's, I skipped ahead of Sharon and Ruby. It had been only a week since Ruby showed me how, and my steps weren't quite right, but it felt good, and besides, it helped me keep up to my longer-legged sisters. We were halfway down the block when I heard Grandma's call.

"Catherine, come back. I must warn you."

My sisters waited while I dutifully returned to hear Grandma's admonition.

"Now Catherine, listen close. Don't leave your sisters—not for one minute. Sometimes naughty men travel with these shows. Hold tight to Sharon's hand. Do you hear me? Don't leave Sharon's side."

"Okay, Grandma. I promise. I'll stay close."

I had no idea what she was talking about, so I quickly turned away and ran down the street after my sisters.

I knew what an elephant was, but I had never seen one. I remembered pictures of a huge animal and wondered if it could be scary like Grandpa's Holstein bull. I was told to never go inside the pasture when the bull was outside, but today we'd see an elephant, and Ruby said she planned to touch its trunk, so it must be nice. Sharon said she wouldn't touch it, but she wasn't brave like Ruby, even if she was two years older.

When Grandma Tregonning gave us our quarters, she said, "It'll cost a dime to get into the show, so you can spend the rest for treats. But don't go into the sideshows. There are things there that little girls shouldn't see. Get a move on now. The main show begins in less than an hour."

When I caught up to Sharon and Ruby, I grabbed Sharon's hand, but Sharon pulled away. "I don't want you clinging on me. Just walk close behind."

I skipped along after them, close enough so I didn't lose sight of Sharon's dress. When I got to Hinton's main street, I turned towards town, but Sharon and Ruby headed in the opposite direction. At first, I was so intent on my footwork that I didn't notice, and by the time I turned back, they were more than a block ahead. I ran to catch up. "You left me behind," I said.

"You'll have to pay attention," Ruby said. "We can't watch you every minute. You don't want to get lost, do you?"

Ruby grabbed my hand and pulled me along.

"How far is it?" I said.

"It's outside of town, out where there's room for tents and animals," Sharon said. "Out past the old cemetery, where we put flowers on the graves."

I remembered helping at the graves last spring, but I had no idea where we'd been. I pulled away from Ruby and trotted along close behind. After a couple more blocks, I thought I heard music, but it was a strange kind of music, a lively music like Father's fiddle music, bouncy music that made me want to skip again. "Do you hear that?" I asked.

"That's a calliope," Sharon said. "I read about it in school. All circuses have them."

"A calipee?" Ruby said. "Never heard of it."

I looked at Ruby in surprise. I thought she knew everything. I sniffed the air as we approached the big tent. It smelled kind of like Grandpa's farm yard, but like Grandma's kitchen when she baked bread, too. I couldn't see any animals, but I saw stands where vendors sold peanuts and root beer. When I saw a man next to a big shiny bowl, I stopped and gawked when he pumped the pedal, and the bowl spun and filled with a fluffy, wool-like substance. He stuck a stick in the mix, twirled it, and the fluff grew into a giant ice cream cone. He smiled down at me. "Would you like a cotton candy, little girl? Only a nickel."

Ruby grabbed my hand and pulled me away. "Not now, mister," she said. "Maybe after the show."

She tugged on my hand. "Come along, Catherine."

I resisted for a moment, but then did as she said.

Straining against Ruby's grip, I turned toward Sharon. "Cotton candy. What's that?"

"I had one at the county fair," Sharon said, "Like sugar on a stick, and it sure tastes good."

"It's too sticky," Ruby said.

We approached the ticket master, handed him our quarters, and he returned a dime and a nickel to each of us. "Take any seat," he said.

We rushed along the straw-strewn path to wooden bleachers that faced a single ring. Sharon pointed toward the curved wooden curb. "That's where they perform."

The front bleachers were full, but when we approached, a man and woman left their seats and climbed the steps.

Ruby rushed to the space and sat down. "Let's sit here, up front where we can see good."

Sharon and I weren't discouraged when the woman behind said, "You're going to get wet, little girls."

For the next hour, the ringmaster, clowns, animals, and aerialists entertained the crowd. As we walked out, Ruby flicked water off her brow. "I liked the high wire best."

Sharon shook her head vigorously and admitted, "I shut my eyes."

I giggled as I brushed water from Sharon's dress. "The elephant liked me. She didn't blow her nose in my direction, not even once."

"You were just lucky," Ruby said.

"She wasn't lucky," Sharon said. "Catherine ducked behind me every time she blew."

I jutted out my chin and snickered while proclaiming, "Sometimes it's good to be little. I liked all the animals. The elephant was really big, lots bigger than Grandpa's bull." I heard the elephant trumpet and turned back to watch as handlers led the animal around the big tent. "I liked the horses best. I'd like to be the pretty lady on the horse."

"She was indecent," Sharon said. "Mama'd skin you alive if you went outside undressed like that."

"Dad would skin you if you tried standing on Fanny's back," Ruby said.

I skipped ahead and then turned and stuck my tongue out at Ruby. "I'll do it someday, just wait and see."

A crowd filled the narrow paths outside the big tent. So many people milled about that I couldn't see my way. Some played the carnival games, and others stood in line waiting for food. I smelled freshly popped corn, but I couldn't see over the people.

Ruby grabbed my hand, and we followed Sharon who had a homing instinct for food. "I'm going to buy a cotton candy," Sharon said as she nudged her way to the end of the longest line.

"Might as well eat sugar," Ruby replied. "It's too sweet."

"I want some peanuts," I said. "I want to feed the animals."

"You'll spend Grandma's money on the animals?" Ruby asked.

"I'll share." I remembered that Grandma had told us we should share because she didn't have many toys at her house. "Grandma likes us to share."

"Not with animals," Ruby said. "I'm thirsty. I want a root beer."

Food in hand, we pushed through the crowd to where the animals were tied behind the big tent. I fingered my nickel and pennies as I pushed them deep into my pocket. "I have more money than you," I told Ruby.

"The peanuts cost less," Ruby said, but she didn't seem to care.

The elephant leaned into her chain and swung her trunk from side to side as I approached. A sign with a long name on it was stuck in the ground. Sharon corrected me when I mispronounced it.

"Her name's Francine," Sharon said.

I stood for a moment, watching my sisters until they stopped to inspect the two camels and the four horses, and then I plopped down just beyond the reach of the huge animal.

I took a peanut, shucked its hull, and stuffed the meats into my mouth. "One for me." Then I lifted my biggest nut from the bag and reached it toward Francine. I wasn't sure whether I should shuck it or not, but Francine didn't seem to care. She trumpeted her thanks as she stretched her trunk to take it. "And one for you." I continued to share my treasure with my new friend until the bag was half-empty. I told Francine all about Grandma's pies, and Mother's food pantry, and my horse, Fanny. I forgot about my sisters until Ruby called, "Come on, Catherine. We're going to the other side."

I jumped up, but before I left, I dug a handful of peanuts from my bag and held them out to my friend, who eagerly accepted the offer. "I'm sorry, but I've gotta go now. It's been nice meeting you," I called back and waved as I turned toward my sisters. Francine trumpeted her thanks as I walked away.

Ruby turned down the path toward the smaller tents, toward the sideshows.

"Grandma said we shouldn't go there," Sharon said. "She said they're not for children."

"Oh, come on, Sharon," Ruby said. "We'll just look at the pictures."

Ruby grabbed my hand and pulled me toward the tents.

Sharon hesitated. "Ruby!" She hollered after us, but when we didn't turn back, she soon followed.

There were big posters pasted on the small tents that showed a fat woman, a very thin man, a bearded lady, and weird animals, but the poster that caught my eye was the one with a man who had red and blue tattoos all over his naked body—terrible writhing lizards and one-eyed gargoyles. They looked like pictures I'd seen of Hell, so I turned away.

We moved down the row of tents until we got to where a barker called to the crowd. "He prances and dances, cavorts on a string. Throw him a penny and maybe he'll sing."

Sharon looked up at a large poster that hung behind the barker, a poster that showed a giant puppet. She read aloud, "See the man-sized puppet. Is he wood or is he flesh?"

"Puppets aren't big. They can't sing," I said. I remembered the Punch and Judy shows where little people batted each other with sticks.

"They don't sing," Sharon said. "It's someone behind the curtain."

"Let's go in," Ruby said.

No!" Sharon said. "Grandma told us to not go in the sideshows." She turned away.

But Ruby handed her nickel to the barker. "Grandma won't care if we go to a puppet show. Come on, Catherine." She pulled me along.

I reached my nickel toward the man.

"Ruby," Sharon hollered. "Grandma. . ."

But Ruby had already pulled me into the tent.

Sharon followed.

We walked toward a small stage that was surrounded by gaudy red, yellow, and green painted panels. A blue curtain ran across the back, and another was pulled to each side at the front. Ruby pushed through adults to the front row of a small set of bleachers, to seats already filled by a group of men who, at first, ignored her. She stopped in front of them and, hands on her hips, stared into their faces. They didn't seem to notice, but when she continued to stare, one said to his friend, "Looks as if the young ladies need a seat." He grabbed his friend's arm and stepped to the next level. "Be a gentleman, Zeb. Let the ladies have the front seats."

The men moved up and started to sit when a man already planted there said, "Hey, watch my fedora." He then stumbled as he rose, regained his balance, snatched his hat, and walked his hands along the wooden seat as he staggered three steps over, right behind where I sat down.

I smelled beer and covered my nose as I lowered myself to the plank. Ruby and Sharon squeezed in beside me, pushing me over to where I was the direct target of the drunk's foul breath and random clumsiness. I leaned forward.

Ruby looked back, scowled, and said, "I hate beer smell." She nudged me, and I was about to agree with her, but then music started to play, and a man-sized puppet stumbled onto the stage. His arms were attached to thin ropes that were tied to his shoulders, elbows, and hands that flapped wildly. Similar ropes fixed to his knees seemed to control his spastic movement across the stage. But when I looked at his face, I covered my eyes. He looked horrible. The left side of his face was little more than a tin can with a painted eye overlay. And the right side had skin flaps protruding from a sunken cheek and a depressed jawbone. As advertised, the Puppet Man frolicked to the bubbly piano music.

I concentrated my attention on his legs, which moved out-of-sync with the music. Sharon could dance much better, but she'd be afraid to do it in front of so many people. I wouldn't do it either. I'd never want to be a puppet on a string.

Someone threw a penny, but the Puppet Man didn't notice it bounce across the stage behind him. Another coin flew through the air, hit Puppet Man on the shoulder, and landed at his feet. He stopped, bent over, and picked up the copper, scanned the audience with one hand to his brow. When the music changed, in a voice as tinny as his face, he sang, "Twinkle, Twinkle, Little Star."

I cringed, but I took a penny from my pocket and held it out. At first the performer didn't see it, but the man behind Sharon who had given his seat to her, called out, "Hey Puppet Man, the little girl has a penny for you."

Puppet Man stopped, turned back, and stumbled toward where I kneeled and held out my penny. As Puppet Man stooped to take the coin from my hand, the drunk behind me hollered, "Are you as ugly under that mask as you are in it?" The drunk tottered as he leaned over me, chortled, and looked about for approval.

Ruby shouted, "You nasty man," and turned her cup over his head, soaking him with root beer.

The drunk swayed, wiped his eyes, and grabbed at Ruby who fought back with her usual ferocity, and she was assisted by the men alongside who pulled the drunk back and held him down.

When the unkind words blasted through the tent, I thought I heard the Puppet Man squeal and looked up in time to see a tear run down his disfigured face. "Please don't cry, Puppet Man," I said as I pressed the penny into his hand.

He smiled, rose to his feet, and bowed before he continued his dance and song while he crossed the stage.

We left the tent and walked through the circus grounds. Carnies called to the crowd, their many voices assaulting my ears as we strolled along the pathways.

"Throw the ball in the basket, win a Kewpie doll!"

"Pop a balloon and take a prize home!"

"Ring the bell!"

"I'll guess your age!"

"Take a goldfish home!"

And there were rides, too. "Let's ride on the Ferris wheel," Ruby said. "I've never been so high."

Sharon agreed, but somewhat reluctantly. She wasn't brave like Ruby.

Ruby pulled me along, but I resisted. "I don't want to go. I'm afraid."

"You can sit between us," Sharon said. "We'll hold onto you."

"No!"

"Just leave the 'fraidy cat," Ruby said.

"We can't leave her," Sharon said. "Grandma would skin us."

"Then she'll just have to come," Ruby said. "I'm going to fly in the sky."

But I was adamant. "I'll not go."

The attendant called, "Are you going with us or not, girls?"

"Okay, you can stay," Sharon said, "but wait right here until we come down. Promise?"

"I'll wait," I said. And I did. I watched the giant wheel go around and around, Ruby and Sharon waving from on high, but I got dizzy and turned away.

For a while, I watched people walk up and down the path. I walked a few paces away from the ride and tried to see the animals behind the tent, but didn't go far enough to catch a glimpse. I stood by the entrance to the giant wheel and counted, but got mixed up past five hundred, so I stopped counting and watched people again. And when I saw Sharon's pale blue, flowered print dress move down the path away from me, I knew that I'd daydreamed, forgotten my sisters, and almost missed their departure. I ran along behind until I saw the tethered animals ahead. When I got to the horses, I slowed and called, "Sharon, can I watch the horses?"

But Sharon didn't answer.

I called again. "Sharon, can I stay with the horses?"

The distance between us increased, but Sharon never turned back.

"Sharon!" Why didn't she stop? I ran after my sister. I caught up and grabbed her dress. "Sharon, I called you."

When she turned around and pulled away, I knew it was a mistake. There was a stranger in Sharon's dress.

I ran back toward the animals, and then, confused, I paused. Two paths led around the tent, and I wasn't sure which one to take.

I stood at the junction and looked down the paths to see if my sisters might be coming, but I saw no one I knew. Tears trickled down my cheeks, but I didn't utter a sound. Daddy told me to be a brave knight whenever I scrubbed my knee and it hurt, and I wanted to be brave, so I stifled my tears. Then I heard a voice call from behind a small tent.

"Little girl. Are you hurt?" A man's head stuck out from the canvas.

"I can't find Sharon and Ruby."

"Are you lost?"

"I can't see my sisters."

"I've got a puppy. Would you like to see my puppy? You can pet him while you wait for your sisters."

I knew that I shouldn't go with strangers. I remembered Grandma Tregonning's warning: "Stay close to Sharon and Ruby."

But I couldn't find them.

I stood where I could see lots of people walking the two paths, but I didn't see Ruby or Sharon. "I won't leave here, not 'till they come."

"He's the prettiest little puppy you've ever seen," the voice called. "Why, I think your sisters are petting him right now." His head disappeared for a moment but popped back out, and he showed a rope to me. "Oh, he's such a cute puppy." He tugged on the rope as if he were pulling his dog. "Your sisters are bigger than you, aren't they?"

"Sharon and Ruby?" I said and started in the man's direction.

He disappeared into the tent, and I heard him say, "Back here, little girl. Pet the puppy. Back here with Sharon and Ruby."

When I reached the canvas, a hand grabbed my arm and tugged me through the opening. I resisted and stumbled, but the man grinned and pulled harder. And when I saw there was no puppy and didn't see my sisters, I screamed, "You're hurting my fingers!" The man covered my mouth with one hand and pulled me inside the tent with the other. Then, as he took hold of my dress, a hand reached into the tent, grabbed him by the hair, and yanked both him and me back into the sunlight.

I gasped. It was Puppet Man. The stranger released me and tried to scramble away, but Puppet Man held tight. He twisted the stranger's arm behind his back and yanked it up, hard. The man screamed, but Puppet Man didn't let loose his grip. Instead, he turned to me and said, "He's a bad man, little girl," and twisted harder. I began to cry. I didn't want to be brave. I wanted Ruby and Sharon.

When he saw me crying, Puppet Man released the stranger and dropped to his knee in front of me. He took my hand. "It's okay, little girl. Please don't cry. I remember, you gave me a penny."

I tried to smile. "And I told you not to cry."

Puppet Man smoothed my hurt fingers, and I felt safe. I smiled as he took a folded hanky from his pocket and dabbed at my tears.

"What's your name, little girl?"

"It's Catherine, and I'm staying with my grandmother, Grandma Tregonning."

He dropped my hand. "Tregonning?"

A call trumpeted down the path. "Jesse, get away from that girl."

Puppet Man jumped up. "Mr. Heinzelman."

I thought Puppet Man looked scared.

Heinzelman rushed up, Sharon and Ruby right behind. He grabbed Puppet Man's shoulder. "What did you do to that girl?"

Ruby grabbed me. "Why did you run away? We told you to wait."

Sharon shook me. "We saw you leave, but we were at the top of the big wheel, and when we screamed, you didn't stop. And the man wouldn't let us off until the ride was over." She shook me harder. "I'll never take you any place again."

Puppet Man jerked away from Heinzelman and ran. When I saw the fear in his face and his panicked departure, I knew it was all my fault. I wanted to defend him, but I couldn't say the words. I cried like I'd never cried before. I didn't care what Daddy said. I didn't want to be a brave knight. Not this time.

2

RUBY BATTLES THE ST. MARY'S BOYS

Author's Note

Mother grew up during the depression years when life was difficult for everyone. Some didn't have food to feed their families. Although my mother's family struggled to meet their needs, they had enough food, much of it produced in their garden. And, although they lived in town, they kept a cow for milk and chickens for eggs and meat.

Mother and Alice walked to school and back home each day, and often they walked home for lunch. She wrote in *From High on the Bluff*, "I went to kindergarten, and first and second grade in the upper ward school. Alice and I had to walk about three-fourths of a mile to school. For third, fourth, fifth, and sixth grade, I went to the lower ward school, which was just as far to walk."

She told how they had to run the gauntlet past St. Mary's school where the boys, knowing their route, would wait in hiding to ambush them. Alice found ways to thwart the attacks, and Mother relied on her sister for protection.

I expanded Mother's account in this short story, telling how Ruby protected Catherine.

I didn't like Ruby's bossiness, but I learned that was the price to pay for protection. Many a time, she protected me at a cost to her own body. The first time I remember was the day she confronted those awful St. Mary's boys.

Ruby always had a plan, and I was her willing accomplice.

I was nine years old, and Ruby was eleven. "Now Catherine, you wait here and I'll walk alone past St. Mary's. They'll be waiting behind the shrubs, but when they pop out, I'll head down Davis Street and outrun them. Then when all's clear, you run past the school. But run fast 'cause they'll be back soon."

"But, Ruby, what if they catch you?"

"They never have yet. Count to fifty, then run fast." Ruby thrust her lunch into my hands. "Here, take my sack. It'll only slow me down. Meet me in front of the Methodist Church."

Twice a day, we had to get past those terrible boys at St. Mary's school. Sometimes they put rocks in the snowballs, and those hurt. But I knew that Ruby could outrun them. So I waited until I heard shouting in the distance and knew they were after her, so I counted. I counted faster when I heard Ruby's loud voice. And when I reached fifty, I ran my fastest and didn't stop when I heard screams from far down Davis Street.

Usually Ruby beat me there, but when I got to the Methodist Church, I didn't see her. I waited and worried. If they caught her, what would those awful boys do? I remembered the circus and that nasty man. I walked around the church twice because I didn't know what else to do. She should have been here by now. I was just about to go inside to find Reverend Leonard when I saw her coming. She looked awful: Her hair hung loose, her coat was covered with snow, and she had scratches on her face. I shouted, "What did those boys do to you?" But she didn't even answer. I could see that she was as mad as a wet hen. "Ruby, are you okay?"

"You think I look bad, you should see that Rodney Clagmire. I bloodied his nose and tore the buttons off his coat. And Billy Langdon ran back toward St. Mary's crying. They'll think twice before they tackle me again."

"But, Ruby, how'd they ever catch you?"

"I slipped on a patch of ice."

"Why are boys so nasty?"

"You know what they say," Ruby said. "Snakes and snails and puppy dogs tails—that's what little boys are made of."

"I'd rather have the puppy dog."

I liked third grade. Ruby said that she liked fifth grade, too, but her teacher didn't read poetry like our teacher did for us. Every morning, first thing, Mrs. Day read a poem, and today she read one of my favorites, "The Village Blacksmith" by Longfellow. It reminded me of the muscles in Daddy's arms when he wrenched a wheel hub off an old Tin Lizzie.

Under a spreading chestnut tree
The village smithy stands;
The smith, a mighty man is he,
With large and sinewy hands;
And the muscles of his brawny arms
Are strong as iron bands.

The morning speeded by until we got to math class, but then it slowed a little. I didn't much like math.

All the grade school students got together in the basement lunchroom at noon, so I sat with Ruby. Mom had filled my bag with more than I wanted to eat: a ham sandwich, watermelon pickles, a piece of apple pie, and a jar of plum preserves. She said we needed to store energy for these cold days. I thought that I already had enough, but maybe she was right. Maybe I'd run faster if I ate it all. Ruby ate hers.

I noticed that Esther Wainwright sat alone in the corner, and she wasn't eating. But I could see that she'd been crying. Esther was kind of shy, and she didn't have many friends, so I felt sorry for her. "Ruby, I'm going to sit with Esther," I said. "She's all alone, and she looks sad." But Ruby was so busy telling Nancy Cramer about her fight with the boys that she didn't even notice me leaving.

Esther smiled as I approached. "May I sit with you?" I said.

She didn't say anything, but she nodded, so I thought it was okay. "Esther, where's your lunch?"

At first, she didn't answer.

"Did you eat it already?"

And when she began to cry, I knew she didn't have a lunch.

"Oh, Esther, would you like some of mine? Mom makes way too much, and I can never finish it all. She gets upset when I bring it back home, and I hate to throw food away. Would you help me?"

"We don't have much food in the house, not until Dad gets paid next week. I get so hungry."

I broke my sandwich into two pieces. "Here, you eat these." I shoved half a sandwich, a pickle, and my apple pie across the table. But I kept my plum preserves; I really liked plum preserves. "You'll be helping me out. Mom'll be happy that I finished everything today."

I could see that Esther appreciated my food. She hardly took a breath between bites.

At supper that night, I told Mom and Dad, "The Wainwrights don't have any food in their house. Esther would have gone hungry today if I hadn't shared my lunch with her."

"Oh, that poor family," Mom said. "They have two children younger than Esther. Will, I'll pull a basket of food from the root cellar. You run it right over there so they can have some supper. And I'll get another basket together for tomorrow."

I knew that Mother would be happy when she heard I'd shared my lunch.

"We may not have a lot," Dad said, "but so many people have nothing these days. We have much to be thankful for."

Ruby came to me after supper and said, "It was nice what you did for Esther today. I was so busy bragging that I didn't even see her. I'm ashamed."

Ruby was like that. Her heart was big, but sometimes she just didn't notice things. And I wished she wasn't so bossy.

3

THE PILFERED SPROUTS

Author's Note

One of the first stories I remember is about the day Mother and Alice short-changed their Great-Uncle Dick when planting his sprouts. She told the story in *From High on the Bluff*, writing, "Sometimes we had to go out in the country with our Great-Uncle Dick to plant pumpkin seeds and potatoes. He gave us twenty-five cents a day and a lunch that his daughter Emma had cooked and put up. As I said before, Emma was one of the world's best cooks, so it wasn't too hard a job for us, given the rewards."

But the day was hot, and they got tired, so Alice suggested a devious scheme. Mother wrote, "Alice always came up with these bright ideas, and I thought she was some kind of god; so I did everything she told me to do."

I'd heard this story many times before Mother wrote her memoir, and she'd always conclude with, "I should have known better."

I think after all those years, she still felt a bit guilty.

Now, I'll tell Catherine and Ruby's version of the story in all its rich detail.

Ruby and I began the day determined to earn money to buy a new dress for our sister, Sharon. You'd think I would have wanted to tell the world that we helped our sister, but I was too ashamed to tell anyone what we did.

Up to this point, when it came to being bossy, Ruby played in the primary grades. But my sister was a fast learner. She may have only been eleven years old, but I think she earned a high school diploma for bossiness. She must have skipped a few grades along the way.

Sharon was kind enough to help me get out of trouble whenever I needed her to. Most of the time, Ruby was the one who got me into the trouble in the first place. I remember the time that Ruby and I tried to help Sharon. And we helped her, but I'm still ashamed of how we did it. I always did what Ruby said, even when I knew she was wrong.

I remember Sharon racing through the kitchen in tears. "Sharon, what's the matter? What's wrong?"

She didn't stop or reply; instead, she rushed up the back stairs.

Our kitchen was big and everything was in place. Mother saw to that, but Sharon helped lots. Sharon deserved a new dress, I thought. She worked hard for the family. And Dad had promised her that dress, but when Ernest O'Doul said he needed medicine for his daughter who had the croup, Dad said he'd wait until next month for the money owed him. During these Depression years, few people had money for repairing their cars, and Dad didn't press too hard when he knew they were desperate.

I followed Sharon to her bedroom. I seldom saw my cheerful sister cry. "What's the matter? Please tell me. Maybe I can help."

"Oh, dear Catherine," Sharon said, "you can't help, not unless you have a treasure secreted away someplace."

"Is it the dress?"

"I've not had a new dress since confirmation. I so wanted one for the school's Spring Ball. My confirmation dress is way too small. I've grown this last year—at the top, you know."

"Mama'll alter it. She's good at that. It'll almost be new."

"Not to me, it won't," Sharon said as she broke into tears once more.

The next morning before church, I told Ruby about the dress, about the broken promise. Ruby didn't respond at first; she paced our bedroom with her head down in thought. "There must be something we can do."

I knew that Sharon would help Ruby or me if we had a problem. Why, Sharon saved my skin many a time. I decided to pray about it during the minister's minute of silence.

When two days later, Cousin Joe said he wanted our help planting potatoes and offered a penny a sprout, I knew my prayers were answered.

This time I'd help Sharon. My father's cousin Joe owned two acres on the edge of town in which he planted potatoes. Usually he hired our older cousins to help, but this year, their father said he needed them at home. And it was a late spring, so Cousin Joe wanted the sprouts planted soon.

Mother said that we could miss one day of school, but no more. If we didn't finish on Wednesday, we'd have to work after school on Thursday and Friday. So we'd have to work fast. Sharon's ball was Saturday night.

The day was hot (over ninety degrees, a record temperature for so early in the season), but I was eager and used to work, so I was certain we could earn enough to buy the dress. We'd never planted that many potatoes, but after careful calculation, Ruby said we could earn fifty cents an hour between us, maybe more. If we worked ten hours, we could earn five dollars, more than we'd ever earned before.

The flat, lightly tilled field stretched out before us. Cousin Joe marked the rows with long strands of binder twine. He pulled a hay wagon loaded with bushel baskets to the fence line and left an eight-gallon milk can of cold water in the wagon's shade. The baskets overflowed with sprouts.

We each grabbed a pail and filled it with sprouts. I started up one row, Ruby another. At first, we worked fast, and I calculated pennies as I dug, set the sprout, and covered it with cool, loose soil. The first hour, we made our fifty cents, each burying twenty-five sprouts. But the farther we went up the field, the longer it took to run back and fill our pails. And the higher the sun got in the sky, the more often we returned for a cold drink of water. Soon we spent half of our time running, and our production dipped sharply.

We dug faster, but that tired us more quickly, so we worked slower. And to make matters worse, the now-hard soil, baked by the sun, made digging more difficult. By noon, I was worn to a frazzle, and my hopes for a five-dollar payday waned. For a while, I sat eating my lunch in silence, too hot and tired to talk. Then, after ten minutes, I rolled over to face Ruby. "Maybe we should be satisfied with less. We'll never get them all planted. I'm beat."

"We'll get that five dollars one way or another," Ruby said. "I'll figure it out, just you see."

"We don't have to finish today," I said. "Cousin Joe said we have all week."

"We'll finish today." Ruby took a swallow from the dipper and flung the remaining water at my feet. "We'll finish today or my name's not Ruby O'Shaughnessy. I promised my friend Rachel that I'd go to the town hall concert after school tomorrow and to our class party Friday night, and I don't plan to miss them. We'll finish these potatoes today."

I knew that Ruby seldom failed when she set her mind to it. I was sure we'd finish planting today, but I didn't know how.

After lunch and a short rest, we attacked the firmly packed soil with renewed vigor, and again, we made fifty cents the first hour. Ruby said, "I told you we'd finish."

But soon it became clear that Ruby hadn't accounted for the afternoon sun. My blouse and slacks hung heavier with each trip I made up the field. Again, I slowed as I recognized the futility of our effort. We'd never earn enough money today.

Ruby called to me. "Don't be so lazy. There's a ton of potatoes left in the wagon." She filled her pail and raced up the row, but I lagged behind.

We worked a while longer but continued to lose ground toward our five-dollar payday. I didn't mind work. It was a part of my young life, but the heat became too much. We'd never get enough money to help Sharon. Even under Ruby's stern glare, I slowed to a halt. Finally, I crawled under the wagon and rested in the shade. My back ached, and my fingers throbbed with pain.

"I thought you cared for Sharon," Ruby shouted as she worked on, but after another half hour, she joined me under the wagon. "Wow, that sun's hot," she said as she took a mouthful of lukewarm water from the dipper. "I've never been so tired."

Ruby sat but remained quiet. I could see that she was deep in thought, so I turned away and laid my head on the ground, certain the sun had won the day. But I'd underestimated Ruby. After a while, Ruby stood and said, "Fill your pail."

I jerked upright. "What?"

"I said, fill your pail."

"Ruby, I can't plant another potato. I'll come back alone tomorrow if I must, but I'll die if I have to plant more today. I'll never get out of bed in the morning."

"Just do as I say," Ruby said as she slammed sprouts into her bucket. "Fill your pail."

I eased off the ground and began to drop potato sprouts into my pail, one at a time. "I can't do this, Ruby. You'll kill me. You'll not have a sister to love you anymore. No one to boss you around." As if I ever did the bossing.

"Oh, shut up, you silly. You'll survive, and we'll get our five dollars. I have a plan."

I dropped a sprout onto the bucket's rim, and, as it bounced to the ground, I glared at Ruby. I knew about Ruby's plans, and most of them got me into trouble. "What are you thinking?"

"Just fill your pail and follow me."

Ruby grabbed her full pail and headed across the field, past the rows marked by twine to the far side, where trees and brambles thrived in the sunlight. At first I hesitated, but then I slowly followed. What did my scheming sister have in mind?

Ruby walked into the woods but stopped by a downed tree. "When we planted the first row today, I noticed this hollow trunk. Do you understand my plan now, sis?"

A hollow log. How could that help? "What are you thinking?"

Ruby didn't answer. She walked to the empty trunk, took a handful of sprouts from her pail, and shoved them inside. "We'll plant these potatoes today even if it's in an old log. Maybe they'll grow like mushrooms. They grow mushrooms in logs, you know."

At first, I stood open-mouthed. "We can't do that. It's cheating. It's dishonest." I took a step toward the wagon but turned back. "I couldn't cheat Cousin Joe. Ruby, I'm ashamed of you."

Ruby grabbed my arm with one hand while she wrenched my pail away with the other. "We worked hard today, Cathy. Cousin Joe would agree with that." She pushed more sprouts into the log. "The working conditions were more severe than we bargained for. You've heard Dad say that wages increase when conditions are harsh." She pushed another handful into the cavity. "We deserve more under these conditions, and this is a way of getting more. You've read how much steelworkers make because they spend all day in front of those hot blast furnaces. It really is fair, sis."

I hadn't thought about it that way. Maybe it did make sense, but if it was fair, we should tell Cousin Joe. When I suggested that to Ruby, she was emphatic. "Oh, no! He might not see it that way. He doesn't have the education or experience with labor that Dad has. We'd best just do it and say nothing. It's okay, Cathy. It really is fair."

I wasn't so sure. I thought that maybe we should tell Dad, but I didn't mention that to Ruby. "I don't know. You're probably right about working conditions, but it doesn't seem fair to not plant Cousin Joe's sprouts. He'll not get all the potatoes he expects when he digs them this fall."

"That's a long time from now. Besides, Cousin Joe really likes Sharon. He'd want to help her get a dress."

Yes, it's true, he was fond of Sharon. But I knew we'd not be knocking on Cousin Joe's door any time soon telling about his contribution to Sharon's dress fund. I should have known better, but Ruby said it was okay. I shivered a bit as I thought about the potatoes Cousin Joe wouldn't get that fall.

Cheating Cousin Joe didn't remain our secret. Dad found out. Joe was nice about it, but Dad wasn't very happy. After a good deal of questioning, he decided that Ruby was the main culprit, so he punished her the most. After settling the score with Joe by contributing a wagonload of hay for his horses, he made Ruby pay by cleaning out our horse stalls for a month. I helped the first week.

And Ruby didn't complain. She was like that. She'd take punishment when she had it coming. But I knew it wouldn't change her ways.

4

THE ELEVENTH COMMANDMENT

Author's Note
Mother told how she and Ruby outsmarted their older brother when he brought good chocolate candy home. She wrote, "At the pool hall, Mort would play the punch boards and win boxes of candy—good chocolate candy. He would bring them home and wouldn't give us girls even one piece. Rather, he would hide them in every conceivable place, like trouser legs hanging in the closet, between the mattresses, behind dressers—any place he thought we might not look. But somehow his sisters would find them. And were they good. And was he angry!"

Because I didn't include a brother in the O'Shaughnessy stories, I recast these events with Ruby and Catherine pursuing their sister Sharon's candy. Ruby convinced Catherine to help by explaining God's Eleventh Commandment. But saving their sister from Hell wasn't as easy as they thought it'd be.

Ruby tried to convince me the Bible had an Eleventh Commandment. I was half-convinced, but I hope God wasn't looking when we did what that commandment suggested.

Before we left Ashley Springs, Sharon began seeing Ed Meadows, a farm boy who lived along Military Ridge, outside Logan Junction. And Ed continued to visit Sharon after we moved to our Wisconsin River farm. We all liked Ed. Dad said he was thoughtful and had a good head on his shoulders. Ruby and I liked him because he brought good chocolates and ice cream for Sharon. But Sharon wasn't very generous. She did her best to hide them from her two younger sisters. But when it came to guile, Sharon was no match for Ruby.

One time, though, I thought Sharon outdid her clever sister. We just couldn't find that candy. I thought we should ask Sharon to be generous, shame her into sharing. But that was far too simplistic for Ruby. Why, Ruby even convinced me that the Commandments required Sharon to share with her sisters, and that justified our larceny. I'd studied those Commandments all my young life, and I'd not seen any such thing. But Ruby said it was so.

I was twelve years old, and I knew the Third Commandment. "Thou shall not steal" was drilled into me from a very young age, first at home and then in Sunday school. Ruby helped me practice my catechism, but she had her own interpretation. "God expects sisters to share," she said. "It's the Eleventh Commandment. God just didn't have room for it on the stone. We'd be saving Sharon by taking her candy."

I didn't remember that in the Bible, but if Ruby said so, then maybe it was true. When Ed brought Sharon a five-pound box of chocolates for her birthday, and Sharon didn't offer any to her sisters, Ruby repeated the Eleventh Commandment and said, "She'll burn in Hell for sure if we don't help her out."

I definitely didn't want my sister to go to Hell, so I followed Ruby to search Sharon's room. To my disappointment, and Ruby's frustration, we couldn't find the chocolates anywhere. I began to think that Sharon might have hidden them outside.

"She wouldn't do that," Ruby said. "She'd not chance that Dad or Petr might find them or an animal getting them. They've got to be here somewhere."

We continued to search—under the bed, in the closet, behind the dressers—but we couldn't find those chocolates.

Ruby said, "Let's think like a detective. What did Sharon do after Ed gave her the candy?"

"She and Ed went to the back parlor. I remember Mom telling them they couldn't shut the doors."

"Okay, let's go downstairs and check the back parlor. Maybe she hid them there."

But we didn't find the candy.

After searching for half an hour, at our wit's end, we sat for a while.

"Let's see," Ruby said. "We looked behind the divan, under the big chair, and on top of the corner cabinet. Where else could they be?"

"Maybe there's a loose floor board," I said. "That's where bandits hide their loot."

"No, they stow it in a hollow tree, or dig a hole or something," Ruby said.

"Well, there's no tree in here," I proclaimed as I tapped my toe across the floor. Finding no loose boards, I sat on the cedar chest and fumed.

"We're going about this wrong," Ruby said. "Let's watch Sharon closely. She'll go to the candy sooner or later. We can follow her and find it."

That night after supper, far too early for bed, Sharon slipped up the stairs. Ruby and I waited a few moments, and were about to follow, when mother called, "Girls, I need help stretching this quilt on the rack. Please give me a hand. The ladies are coming over tomorrow to sew."

Foiled, I thought, just when we were on the trail. Maybe God wasn't so intent on this commandment after all. Ruby gave me a knowing look and nodded in Sharon's direction, but I knew we'd have to help mother. There'd be no chocolates for Ruby and me tonight.

The next night, Sharon left us again, this time excusing herself from the Chinese checker game we were playing. Mom and Dad didn't seem to think this strange, but I knew my sister had evil intentions. We'd have to act soon if we were going to save her from fire and brimstone.

After Sharon returned, she and Mother set to boiling potatoes for the next morning's cold fries. Ruby and I excused ourselves, saying we were tired and wanted to be well-rested for the long day of field work tomorrow.

When we got to the top, Ruby said, "You stand watch here by the stairs, and I'll search Sharon's room again. It has to be there someplace."

Twenty minutes passed before Ruby re-entered the hall. "I can't find those chocolates anyplace," she said. "I looked through her drawers, for a loose board under the carpet, even outside the window, but I couldn't find them."

We continued to search for half an hour but it looked as if Sharon had outsmarted us this time.

Several days passed, during which Sharon continued to climb the stairs more than usual; but try as we might, we couldn't find her loot.

For Ruby, it became an obsession. "I don't care if the box is empty. It's up there someplace, and I'm going to find it if it's the last thing I ever do."

Finally, we caught a break. While we were in the field helping Dad harvest beans, I stepped into a gopher hole and twisted my ankle.

"Help her back home, and soak her foot in Epsom salts," Dad told Ruby. "It doesn't seem too bad, but she should stay off it for a couple days."

Ruby helped me into the house and sat me on a chair while she pumped water, heated it on the cook stove, and searched for the Epsom salts. My ankle hurt like Billy blue blazes, and I wished that Mother was here to help, but she'd gone to tend to old Mrs. Angstrom, who was down with the gout.

"I wonder where Sharon is." I said. "I thought she'd be getting supper ready by now."

Ruby continued to look for the Epsom salts while the water heated. "I think I'll get you upstairs to your bed so you can keep that ankle elevated," she said as she wiggled under my arm and helped me off the chair.

When we reached the top of the back stairs, I heard footsteps down the hall. To my surprise, I saw Sharon rush from our room and down the front stairs. She didn't see us.

"That's strange," Ruby said. "Why was she in our room?"

Ruby helped me down the hall, into our room, and onto my bed. She elevated my foot with two pillows and left, saying, "I'll bring the water as soon as it's hot. Keep that foot up."

Upon returning, she helped me sit on the bed's edge, and I eased my foot towards the water. "Is it too hot?" she said. "I don't want to burn you."

Ruby could be considerate when she took a mind to it. I tested the water before plunging my foot to the bottom. "It's hot, but not too hot. Feels good."

Ruby sat next to me but said nothing for a while.

"I've been thinking," she finally said. "Why was Sharon in our room? I thought I'd see her downstairs when I got there, but she didn't come into the kitchen. Something's rotten in Denmark, Cathy."

I raised my foot from the water. "Gets kinda hot after a while. What do you mean, Ruby?"

"Why would Sharon be in our room? She never comes into our room. You don't suppose she hid the candy in here, do you?"

I eased my foot back into the water. "How sneaky of her," I said. "She wouldn't be that tricky, would she? Not Sharon."

Ruby searched around the room but found nothing. "If she did hide it in here and we found it, wouldn't that be convenient?"

"That'd be too easy for us. I don't think she'd hide it here."

"Maybe, but think how long we've looked without finding it. Maybe she's really being clever about it. If we hadn't seen her leave, we'd never have thought it was here. Let's keep searching."

I withdrew my foot and began to stand.

"Not you," Ruby said. "You soak that ankle. I'll look."

Ruby searched while I thought about places it might be, but after half an hour of soaking, thinking, and searching, we were no closer to the candy—or so I thought. It wasn't until Ruby reached into the back of our closet and vigorously separated our winter clothes that we got a break.

"I heard something," Ruby said. "Did you hear it?"

Ruby shook the clothes again, and the noise was loud and clear. She pushed the pants and blouses on the lower hanger aside and traced the sound upward, up to where winter shirts and jackets hung from the top hangers. Ruby pushed a coat aside, and a big box fell to the floor. "Eureka!" she shouted. "That devious sister of ours never thought we'd look through our winter clothes, not here in our own room. I think we're about to save her from Hell and damnation."

Ruby and I each enjoyed a chocolate-covered cherry.

"Boy, Ed sure is generous," Ruby said as she savored her fruit-filled candy. "He buys the best. No wonder Sharon keeps it to herself."

"We better not take more, not now anyway," I said. "You know what Cousin Gusta told us that Texans say about greedy people?"

"What?"

"Pigs get fed, hogs get slaughtered."

Without a word of protest, Ruby gently lifted the two empty wrappers and rearranged the candies that were left in the box. My headstrong sister accepted Gusta's advice, even from a thousand miles away.

That night, my ankle felt some better, so I limped down to dinner. I didn't dare look Sharon in the eye for fear my face would reveal my guilt. Then I remembered what Ruby said about doing God's will, so I felt a little better—but not much.

Sharon didn't notice the missing candy right away.

Several days passed, and Ruby and I continued God's work, but I still felt guilty. As the box emptied, we became adept at camouflaging our larceny, moving and stretching wrappers.

I knew if we continued our thieving ways we'd be found out, but I couldn't stop. I thought about Eve whenever I secretly munched on the chocolate.

The day of reckoning arrived with a screech and an accusation. "Mama!" Sharon screamed. "Ruby and Catherine have been stealing my chocolates!"

I was sure we were in big trouble now, but I underestimated Ruby's cunning. When Ruby said, "It's not our fault, Mama," I supposed she'd tell Mother about the Eleventh Commandment. Instead, she said, "We thought that Sharon wanted to share her chocolates because she left them in our room. Catherine and I talked about it and agreed that if we had chocolates we'd give some to her, so we figured that's what she wanted. She's always been a generous sister." Then she turned to Sharon, and with a smile so wicked I cringed said, "Thank you, Sharon. They sure were good."

Sharon turned as red as the cherries inside her candy, but she didn't utter a word.

I couldn't wait to write Cousin Gusta about Ruby's cunning. I knew she'd appreciate the cleverness of her most ardent protégé.

5

ALL'S WELL THAT ENDS WELL

Author's Note

Mother told many experiences that fueled this next story. She told about Alice racing her horse, a race that resulted in a runaway. She told how she and Alice won when participating in the Lyceum competition. And she wrote the poem that I include in this episode.

This action scene shows the multifaceted Ruby: conniving, fearless, confident, talented, protective, and considerate. On this day, Ruby defends Catherine when Henry attacks her, stands up for her when she loses a talent competition, and stops Henry from whipping his horse.

If I hadn't lived it, I never would have believed a day could be so chaotic.

You'd think by now Ruby should have known that God was keeping an eye on us, that He'd make us pay for every misdeed we committed. But Ruby didn't think that way. She tempted God far more than I liked. Or maybe she couldn't help herself. I think she was addicted to trouble-making. But this time, I think she ended the day in God's favor—and in Dad's, too.

I could hardly sleep. All I could think about was the next day. We were excited and anxious at the same time. At least I was. I don't think anything scared Ruby.

I called to her. "Ruby, aren't you nervous about tomorrow?"

"I've sung 'Dixie' since I was five years old. I could sing it in my sleep. I thought you'd sing, too. You're better than I am."

"Maybe I should have, but I'm afraid I'd go flat or forget the words. I can't face a crowd. I wish I had your confidence."

"You'll do fine. Your poem's a real laugher, and you wrote it yourself. I bet you'll have the only original composition there."

"I tried to write like Edgar Guest. I love his 'It takes a heap o' livin' in a house to make it home.' I think the title is 'Home,' but I like the 'heap o' livin'' part best. Do you think it's okay that I copied him? That's not plagiarism, is it?"

"You didn't copy him, sis. You just copied his style."

"It's okay then? They call him the 'People's Poet,' and I think he is. I know that some don't think highly of him, but I do. But no one's as good as Emily Dickinson. She's my favorite poet."

"They'll love it."

"Well, I can't go flat reciting a poem. And if I forget my lines, I'll have a copy up my sleeve. I'll read it if I have to."

"Don't worry."

"That's easy for you to say, but Ruby, I'm glad you'll be there. You'll know what to do if I faint."

I heard, "Don't worrrry, Cath. . ." and then heavy breathing. Ruby wasn't about to stay awake battling my demons.

An hour later, after what seemed like a hundred recitations of my poem, "Weather Report," fatigue trumped anxiety, and I dozed off.

We were up at sunrise, ready for morning chores, but we didn't accomplish much. Ruby slipped over from the calves she was feeding to ask, "Are you wearing the blue taffeta dress that Grandma gave you last Christmas?"

"This will be the first time I've had a chance to wear it. I can't believe Marge Carlton didn't want it after Grandma made it. It's so beautiful, and it fits perfectly."

"I should have been so lucky. If I were a size smaller, she'd have given it to me. I'm the oldest."

"You're older. Sharon is the oldest."

"It's way too small for Sharon. I'll have to wear her prom dress. It's too big, but Mom says she'll take it in while we're in school today."

I smiled for the first time that morning. "Don't be jealous, Ruby. You'll look fantastic in Sharon's dress, and it's a good thing there's enough room for underskirts and crinoline. You'll look like a Southern belle in your hoop skirt." I curtsied, and my hair almost touched my shoes.

"With that stars and bars banner over your shoulder, it'll be perfect to sing 'Dixie.' You'll win first prize."

Dad pulled a watch from his pocket and hollered across the barn. "You better hurry up, girls. You don't want detention for being late on the first day of the new semester, now do you?"

We hustled through our chores and hurriedly hooked old Mabel to the sled. Maybe Dad should have pushed us sooner as our dalliance set off a series of events that produced a riotous day.

We owned a beautiful little cutter, just like those in a Currier and Ives picture, and there weren't many of those around anymore. Mabel may have been slow as mashed potatoes through a sieve, but she was reliable. Dad and Mom never worried when we were out with Mabel. They knew we'd get home safely.

We could see that the school yard was empty, which was a sure sign the bell had rung or was about to. We stopped abruptly at the one-horse shed that Dad had rented for our use. I jumped off the cutter to the right, Ruby to the left. We each unhooked a trace, grabbed a shaft and slid it from the loops, and then pushed the cutter away from Mabel.

Ruby gasped for air. I must have been in better shape. "The bell hasn't rung yet," she said. "I can see Henry leaning out the window. Hurry, Cathy."

Ruby rushed Mabel into the stall while I shuffled alongside and unhooked her bridle. I broke open a bale and scattered hay into the feed bin while Ruby slipped a halter over Mabel's head and tied it to the stall. Then we rushed from the shed toward the school door.

Before we'd taken ten steps, Ruby shouted, "I forgot her bridle. Go back and get it." She must have thought I was her servant or something, but I didn't protest. I was used to it. I did an abrupt U-turn, retrieved the bridle, slammed the barn door, and caught up with Ruby as she started up the steps. We always took the bridle into the school and hung it with our coats so that Mabel'd have a warm bit in her mouth when we left for home.

We'd not made the top step when a chorus erupted from above. Five boys, led by Henry Schultz, stuck their heads out the window and sang three lines of "The Old Gray Mare."

Then Henry began his own verse. "Oh the old gray mare / she ain't what she used to be / pooped on the whiffletree / pooped on O'Shaughnessy

/ Ohhh—" Before he could finish his crude rendition, a hand snatched him back from the window.

"Well!" I exclaimed.

"I'll get that Henry," Ruby said.

The bell hadn't rung.

We rushed past the principal. We didn't want to attract his attention, but we failed. "You're going to have to milk faster, girls. I can't hold the bell every day."

"I'm sorry, Mr. Pagenkopf," I said. "We'll try to get here sooner."

Ruby scowled.

I popped a stick of gum in my mouth as I headed down the hall for the first day of second semester freshman literature. Ruby noticed. Before entering her study hall, she hollered, "Don't let Mr. Smith catch you chewing gum. He'll make you wear it on your nose the whole class period. My nose is still sticky from last year."

I pulled the gum from my mouth and put it back in the wrapper, saving it for later. I wanted to get off to a good start with Mr. Smith, but I couldn't keep my mind off my poem. I'd repeated it so many times that it popped into my head at the slightest thought of weather. I looked out the window at the snow on the ground—"How ja like this kind of weather?" I saw Jenny's gloves peaking out from her purse— "How ja like the mercury low?" I looked at the U.S. map that hung in front of the room— "Doncha think you'd whole lot rather / be down South where the taters grow?"

I tried my hardest to concentrate, but it was no use. The day dragged. I could only think of the contest. My mind was so befuddled that I made the awful mistake of challenging Mrs. McGurdle in civics class. No one challenged Mrs. McGurdle and lived through it. Everyone knew that she adored Mr. Lincoln more than any president, more than anyone, alive or dead. But when she told us that Abe Lincoln was a great man because he'd freed the slaves when he issued the Emancipation Proclamation, I said, "No, Mrs. McGurdle."

She dropped her chalk and stared with a disdain that wilted the pansies on my dress. After what seemed forever, she said, "You don't think that Lincoln was a great man, Miss O'Shaughnessy?"

The room went silent for everyone but me. My ears buzzed. What was I thinking? What had I done? But it was too late now. The challenge had been issued. "No, Mrs. McGurdle. I mean, Mrs. McGurdle, he was a great man, but the Emancipation didn't free any slaves, not then anyhow."

"Miss O'Shaughnessy, you'll research the Emancipation and bring a complete report to my office Friday after school."

Thank heaven—off the hook, at least for now. With the night's performance in front of me, Friday seemed forever away. And like Scarlett O'Hara, I'd think about it tomorrow.

But the Emancipation wouldn't be postponed so easily. Henry Schultz would see to that. During lunch hour, Ruby and I crossed the street to feed Mabel, and as we returned to school, Henry and his friends met us at the curb.

Henry confronted me while the other freshman boys distracted Ruby. "Catherine O'Shaughnessy, you weren't so smart today with old Gurdle, were you? She's probably sorry they skipped you ahead to ninth grade. Maybe she'll put you back in eighth where you belong."

"You're mean, Henry. Besides, Mom has books that say the Proclamation didn't free slaves when it was issued. Lincoln had no authority in the South, and he wouldn't risk losing political support by freeing slaves in the North or the border states. I'll write that in my report."

But Henry wouldn't quit. "You're dead when you cross old Gurdle. What are you anyway, a rebel sympathizer? You'll get what you deserve." Then Henry picked up a fistful of snow and pushed it in my face.

He'd begun to turn away when a missile knocked him flat. Ruby was on him like molasses on a pancake. After a moment, she leaned over Henry as he cowered in a snow drift. "You little Kraut. Your family fawned over the Kaiser while our uncle died fighting for Lincoln. Don't you ever call us rebel sympathizers again or you'll think that snow is a feather tick compared to what I'll give you next time."

Ruby's timeline was a bit strained, but at that moment, Henry wasn't concerned about trivial distinctions. He was white as the snow drift he tried to crawl away from. "Come on, Ruby, I was joking. I didn't mean anything by it. Where's your Irish sense of humor?"

Ruby hovered above Henry like a hawk over a field mouse. She glared down on him. "I save my Irish humor for humorous people, and you're not humorous; you're pathetic. And Henry, I don't want to hear any more crude songs either."

The other boys grabbed Henry's legs and pulled him away from Ruby. His bravery increased with each foot of separation. "You mean songs about your old mare? She is slow, isn't she, guys?" They all nodded agreement as they backed further away.

Ruby pressed forward. "You think she's slow, Henry? She can beat your old plow horse any day of the week."

"Oh, come on, Ruby, she wouldn't have a chance against Kaiser."

Henry raised his upper body from the snow. The other boys, from a safe distance, nodded. I nodded, too, but Ruby wouldn't back down. "You still tout your Kaiser, do you? Well, our old American horse can whip your Kaiser's fanny any time, any day."

I thought Ruby's patriotic fervor got a bit out of hand, but she was more committed to the cause than I.

Henry's face turned red. I suppose even a mouse fights back sometimes. "You say so, do you? Well, talk's cheap. Let's see who's faster." He spat into the snow at Ruby's feet. "I'll race you home after the talent show. We'll race from the community center to my turn-off. The loser has to bring pastries to the winner every day for the rest of the week."

"That's a deal," Ruby said. "I'll sure enjoy the Kaiser's sweets."

On the way home from school, I said, "Dad told us never to run old Mabel on the sled. She might collapse and die."

"Don't worry, Cathy, I have a plan."

Ruby always had a plan. And that was my worry.

Because of our upcoming talent competition, Ruby and I didn't do chores that night, but that meant Dad would be in the barn longer than usual, so he and Mom couldn't attend the talent show. I felt guilty, but there was no way around it. Dad wouldn't ask Petr to milk alone, not on a frigid January night.

The talent show participants were to be served potluck before the competition, so Ruby and I left home just as Dad, Mom, Sharon, and Petr sat down for supper. Bundled up over our beautiful dresses, we headed for the barn to hook Mabel to the cutter. But as we entered the horse stalls, Ruby walked past Mabel's stall and entered Fanny Too's. "You're going to take Fanny Too?" I said. "You know Dad doesn't want us to drive her on the cutter."

"He never said we couldn't. He just said that Mabel is more reliable."

Dad loved matched pairs of horses. Fanny Too, old Fanny's daughter and a gray like Mabel, was a bit bigger but ten years younger and faster. "Ruby, is this your plan—to run Fanny Too against Kaiser?"

"It's our only chance. I don't know if Fanny Too can beat Kaiser, but she'll give him a good race."

"Isn't that cheating?"

"Maybe, but you know Henry would cheat us if he could."

"I suppose. But he'll know it's not Mabel."

"I don't think so. They're almost the same size and the same color and markings. Besides, it'll be dark with only a half moon. It's worth taking the chance to shut him up once and for all."

We'd eaten potluck, and the master of ceremonies approached the stage. By lot, Ruby performed fifth, and to my dismay, I was last. I'd have to sit and stew while sixteen other performers preceded me. I'd be a mess by the time it was my turn.

"Don't think about your poem," Ruby said. "Think about how we'll leave Henry Schultz in our dust."

Great—now I had two reasons to be nervous. I wasn't afraid of the race but about what Dad and Mom would say when they found out. And I knew they'd find out.

But Ruby was right. It helped to think about the race. I worked myself into such lather worrying about Dad and Mom that I didn't practice my poem once. Instead, I rehearsed excuses that I'd give them.

I'd tell them that Ruby made me do it.

No, I couldn't put the blame on Ruby. After all, she defended my honor.

I could say that we'd made a mistake. We didn't know it was Fanny Too.

Dad would never believe that.

Maybe I could tell him that Mabel limped when we led her out of the barn, so we took Fanny Too.

That wouldn't fly. He could check Mabel's legs.

I remember Ruby going forward to sing "Dixie." She was beautiful in her Southern Belle dress, and her rich contralto voice dished a serving of black-eyed peas and hominy grits to an enraptured audience. The North's casualties may have exceeded 300,000 in that war, but the antebellum South seemed like a romantic place. Many in the North were still captivated by all things Southern.

My mind raced through many excuses, but none seemed sufficient. Just when I'd decided that I should leave the excuses to Ruby, the Master of Ceremonies, Mrs. Marshall, announced, "For the final performance, Miss Catherine O'Shaughnessy will recite an original poem. Miss O'Shaughnessy."

I stood, smoothed my blue taffeta dress, walked onto the stage, and said, "Thank you, Mrs. Marshall." I looked out at my adversaries. "This is—it's a poem that I wrote on a snow—snowy night that was just about as cold as tonight. I hope you'll like it. I call it 'Weather Report.'"

"How ja like this kind of weather?
How ja like the mercury low?
Doncha think you'd a whole lot rather
Be down South where the taters grow?

How ja like the wind a blowin'?
Plum through your hide a penetratin'.
And it's keeping right on snowin'.
Almost wish you was livin' with Satan.

Just look there, how that snow's a flyin',
This way, that way, every which way.
Aincha sick and aincha dyin',
For the good old month of May.

Spring'll come, er that's the sayin'.
So doncha whine and doncha fret.
Just be waitin', hopin', prayin'.
What you pray for, doncha get?"

Poetry was not high on the preferred entertainment list for these country folks, but they were gracious people, giving me a polite round of applause. Not up to the level received by Ruby's "Dixie" and Jason Jasperson's "Wait Till the Cows Come Home," but respectable all the same. I was glad it was over.

I didn't win a prize, but Ruby won the blue ribbon with six more audience votes than Jason. I was happy for her, but every time someone congratulated her, she'd say, "My sister Cathy should have won. She not only recited a poem, she wrote it. She's the creative one."

I may have blushed, but I didn't mind a bit.

By the time we got through the crowd and bundled up for the trip home, Henry and his friends were outside standing next to Kaiser and his cutter. "You didn't forget our little wager, did you Ruby?"

"Of course not, Henry," Ruby said. "We'll harness old Mabel and meet you back here in fifteen minutes. Don't run away scared."

"Of what?"

In less than fifteen minutes, we returned with Fanny Too and our cutter. Henry looked our horse up and down a couple of times, but he didn't protest. "You don't mind if I bring Roy along, do you? I'd like to have a witness to my victory."

"Not at all, Henry, not at all," Ruby said.

I was too nervous to talk.

Fanny Too had balked when we'd left the comfort of her stall, but with our urging, she moseyed onto the street alongside her competitor. Henry clapped his hands, and we surged forward together. Warm and comfortable from the livery, with no reason to hurry, Fanny Too fell behind as Kaiser raced forward at Henry's shouts. It was an unpromising beginning.

We were a block behind by the time we'd reached the edge of town. But soon, cooled by the frigid air and eager to get home to her warm stall, Fanny Too picked up the pace. As we gained, Ruby shouted encouragement.

Henry grabbed his whip.

Although I'd seen horses whipped in movies, I couldn't believe that any farmer would flog his horse. Dad wasn't easily riled, but when we began driving, he'd said, "If I ever hear that you've thrashed a horse, I'll thrash you." I doubt that he would have, but we weren't about to test him, not when it came to mistreating horses. We didn't even carry a whip in the cutter.

Ruby looked at me and shouted, "Why, that little Kraut! Germany's Kaiser deserved a whipping, but not Henry's Kaiser!" Ruby popped the reins. "Getup, Fanny Too!"

Fanny Too seemed to sense the urgency. She shifted into her next gear and quickly closed on the sled ahead. We pulled alongside Henry and Roy less than a mile outside of town. About to lose the lead, the boys screamed so loudly they probably didn't hear Ruby yell, "Henry, the race isn't important enough to pound on your horse! We aren't using a whip! Don't you, either!"

We raced side by side for another ten minutes. The washboard road shook the sleds as violently as it would a Model T that had lost a tire. I clutched the side as we whipped back and forth. Ruby stood like a chariot driver and shouted, "Let's go, Fanny Too. Give it your all. Getup, girl, getup."

Fanny Too's smooth gait proved superior to Kaiser's frightened one, and we slowly edged ahead and began to pull away.

Henry whipped Kaiser until blood flew from the lashes as the distance between us increased. Looking back, I was sickened by the spectacle.

Ruby glanced back and then pulled hard on the reins. As she slowed Fanny Too, Henry surged ahead. She sank onto the seat, and just above a whisper, she said, "Neither winning nor honor is worth abusing an animal. If we have to lose to save Kaiser, we'll lose."

We didn't say another word all the way home. Dad must have seen Mabel in her stall and known that we'd taken Fanny Too, but he didn't say anything when we got home that night. It was pretty late.

By the next day, everyone in school had heard about the race. Henry started bragging, but Roy shut him up fast when he told that we'd have won the race if we hadn't pulled up. Roy didn't hang around with Henry after that.

At first, Dad didn't mention the race, but two days later while we were doing morning chores, he called us over and said, "You can never know how proud I am of you girls."

He never said more.

After that day, my admiration for my sister was never at a higher level. I could even forgive her for being so bossy.

6

A GOOD DAY ENDS BADLY

Author's Note

Of all the stories Mother told, the ones I heard most often were those about her and Alice harassing their older sister, Anne, especially when she was with a boyfriend. Mother would laugh when she told how they frightened Anne and her boyfriend with firecrackers, and how they tried to steal the ice cream that was given to Anne by a would-be suitor.

Mother wrote, "We had a swing on the wrap-around porch on which my two older sisters very often entertained their boyfriends. (I only included Anne in my stories.) One night, when one was sitting there with a boyfriend, Alice and I threw a firecracker under it—which created considerable anger and confusion, but no injuries. The spot was well chaperoned though, since it was directly in front of my parents' bedroom window."

Another time she wrote, "One time we had a neighbor woman whose son, Joe, was about twenty years older than Anne. Joe, whose mother was pushing the situation, had a crush on Anne, although she had no ideas for him. One time when Anne was sick with the flu, Joe brought a pint of ice cream for her every night. But Anne was too sick to eat it. We had a back room, which in winter was our freezer. Mother had an old washing machine where she would put food, so that's where the ice cream went."

She goes on to tell how she and Alice paid a steep price when they attempted to steal their sister's treat.

I'll combine Mother's accounts into an evening when Ruby and Catherine created mayhem, and I'll elaborate the outrageous details of that day's event.

I've heard that crime doesn't pay, but Ruby proved that idiom false every time she'd tested it, so I had complete confidence in her. But that confidence slipped down my dress and fell through a crack in the floor before I went to bed this night.

Ed and Sharon were getting pretty serious, I think. I liked him and hoped for a wedding. And Ruby liked him, too, but that didn't stop her from instigating trouble. From the time they first met, it seemed that Ed was the perfect target for Ruby's pranks.

I was collecting eggs when I heard Ruby's call from the barn. "Cathy! Cathy! Are you in here?"

"Over here. I'm just about done with the eggs."

Ruby rushed from the barn and raced the twenty paces to me. The dust swirled and tickled our noses as she stomped into the little building. She coughed and gagged, but managed to say, "I heard Mom tell Dad something important. Let's get outta here." She pulled me out the door. "Ed's coming to see Sharon. He'll be here for supper."

"Do you think he's serious? Do you think they'll get married?"

Ruby halted outside the doorway and jammed her hands into her hips. "You silly nilly. Sharon hasn't even graduated from high school. Mom would kill her. You know Mom wants us to have careers before we marry."

I did know that, but I was full of budding ideas. "Maybe they'll elope. Wouldn't that be romantic?"

"Romantic? Repulsive is a better word." Ruby was a world-weary fifteen. "Come down from your books, Cathy. I've got an idea."

Before she told me her idea, we heard Dad as he walked up the lane from the river sloughs where he and our ten-year-old neighbor boy, Junkie Jenkins, had been clearing the setlines of big channel catfish they'd hooked the night before. Without sons of his own, Dad enjoyed Junkie's company.

It was late in the afternoon, so Dad suggested that Junkie should head for home, because his parents would expect him by now. But Dad was about to feed the horses, so Junkie protested.

"If you don't leave now, your mama'll spank you," Dad said. "Should we put a shingle in your pants, again?"

"Don't do that, Mr. Shaughnsy. Mama whacked me with the last board you put there."

"Well, we'll have to change strategy, now won't we? I've got an old Farmer's Almanac in the milk house. She wouldn't whack you with the farmer's bible, now would she?" Dad chuckled as they entered the milk house. "Besides, it's sat there so long there can't be much whack left in it. Let's hurry and feed those horses."

As they went off, I straightened the towel over the egg basket and started toward the house. I hoped that Ruby had forgotten her plan.

Whenever Ruby said she had a plan, I got nervous. Ruby's plans usually meant trouble. But even when I knew better, Ruby would convince me to cooperate. I thought she was my personal goddess or something, and she cheerfully took advantage of the fact.

She fell in beside me. "So here's what we'll do."

"I've gotta take these eggs to Mother." I walked faster. "She wants them for dinner."

Ruby grabbed my arm. "No, listen. Remember those firecrackers that Petr fired off on the Fourth?"

"We can't—"

"I heard him tell Dad he has some in his closet that he's saving for New Year's Eve. While they're milking, let's sneak in and take a couple. Then tonight, when Sharon and Ed are on the porch swing, bam!"

I pulled my arm away. "Ruby, we can't go into Petr's room. Mama would kill us if she found out we'd gone into a man's room."

"She won't know."

I started to walk away.

"Okay, you don't have to go in his room; I will. You can stand watch in the hall. I'll find the firecrackers."

"But that would be stealing."

"We'll only need one or two. He'll never miss them."

As I ran toward the house with the eggs, I called back, "I'll think about it."

But I knew that, as always, I'd be at Ruby's side when the dastardly deed went down. I couldn't resist the excitement of a life of crime under Ruby's tutelage, even though I had the heart of a coward. And worse still, Ruby knew it, too.

Sharon helped mother prepare supper, and Ruby and I did our outdoor chores. I rode Fanny Too bareback down the lane to the pasture where the cows fed during the day. With our dog Teddy's help, I herded the cows back to the barn. Now that cold weather had set in, the pasture grass was sparse, so the cows were halfway home by the time I started after them. They were eager to feed on the rich alfalfa that Ruby had forked into the manger.

While we fed the chickens, Ruby unfolded details of her plan. "Dad and Petr just went into the barn. They'll be there for an hour. Sharon and Mom are in the kitchen." She glanced toward the barn, and then at the house. "After we change for supper, you watch the stairs while I slip into Petr's room. If you hear anyone approaching, whistle. If someone comes, we'll hurry back to our room. Okay?"

"I'll not come into Petr's room to ask if you heard my whistle. I'll whistle once, and then I'll run for it."

"You little coward. Next time I'll ask Junkie to help. He may be small, but he's not a 'fraidy-cat."

Ruby brought the firecrackers back to our room where she hid them in the drawer beneath her underclothes. "See how easy it was," she said. "You needn't been scared. I planned it all out."

As Ruby and I headed downstairs to supper, we heard a knock on the front door. Sharon, who was a bit flushed, passed us in the hallway on her way to answer. Ruby, not one to miss an opportunity, said, "That must be your white knight, Sharon. Will you give him your garter?"

Sharon got redder. "Ruby, watch your tongue. You know that Ed's an honorable man. Why, he doesn't even swear."

"Dad doesn't swear. Not unless he's really angry."

Sharon flashed an angelic smile. "Ed never swears."

With a devilish smile, Ruby said, "We'll see."

While Ruby and Sharon sparred, Mom opened the door. "Hello, Ed. It's good to see you again."

"Good evening, Mrs. O'Shaughnessy. I stopped at the grocery and bought a couple quarts of ice cream—one vanilla and the other maple nut, Sharon's favorite." He took the sack from under his coat. "It's cold enough so they shouldn't have melted. I thought we could have them for dessert. I know Mr. O'Shaughnessy loves ice cream, too."

"He sure does, but we don't have store-bought often. You know how to make a hit with him."

Ed looked past Mother but wasn't too conspicuous about it. "Is Sharon here?"

"She was on her way to the door, but I think she stopped to clear up a misunderstanding with her sister. Oh, here she is now."

Ed beamed as he handed Sharon the sack. "I brought your favorite treat, maple nut ice cream."

Sharon lit up. "Ed, you're so thoughtful. I'll put it in the back room. Now that the temperature's dropped, we store things in the old clothes boiler."

Sharon took Ed's arm and led him to the parlor. "I'll be just a moment, Ed."

Five minutes later, Dad and Petr came in from the barn. They said their hellos to Ed and headed for the washroom to shed their barn clothes and clean up. As he re-entered the parlor, Dad said, "I hear you brought some ice cream, Ed. I guess you know how to court a future father-in-law, now don't you?"

Ed blushed, and Sharon, who had just returned, said, "Dad, mind your manners."

But Dad was on a roll. "Next time, bring a gallon and maybe we can do some horse trading. I'm mighty fond of ice cream, and I'll still have two daughters left, now won't I?"

Sharon turned deep red. "Dad, stop it."

Mom glared at him, too, and Dad couldn't help but know he'd gone too far. I knew that Mom didn't like to see her girls embarrassed; also, she didn't like to see Dad encourage an early marriage. She had other ideas.

"No offense," Dad said. "I'm just joshing a bit. Everyone sit down and eat so we can get to that ice cream. The house rule is you can reach as far as you're able, but you gotta keep one foot on the floor."

I didn't dare look at Ruby, nor did I look anyone else in the eye either, for fear that a map of my guilty intentions would erupt like acne across my face.

While others exchanged the platters of chicken, mashed potatoes, gravy, green beans, deviled eggs, and hot rolls, Mom said to Dad, "Was the Jenkins boy over this afternoon?"

"Junkie? Yes, he helped me check the setlines and feed the horses. He sure does love the horses."

Ed frowned. "Junkie? That's a funny name. How'd he get that one?"

Mom set the gravy bowl down, right in the dish of potatoes. "Whoops," she said.

Ruby and I didn't even notice until everyone broke out laughing.

"I always put gravy on my mashed potatoes," Mom said. She harrumphed and carefully spooned the potatoes off the bowl. "Oh, yes, Junkie? His mother told me that when Junkie was still crawling around the floor, his oldest brother, Zeke, told their neighbor lady that he was just another piece of junk in the house. And it stuck. He's been Junkie ever since." She set the gravy bowl back down, but more carefully this time. "But Will, you know his father doesn't like him around horses. His uncle was badly injured by a horse."

"How's a boy to learn if he's never allowed around them, Mother? And he does love the animals. We're careful. I never let him in the stall or inside the fence. He feeds them from outside."

Petr, who said little to anyone ever since some bad days fighting in his Polish homeland, set his fork down and looked up from his plate. He stared across the table—right at me. I knew that he knew. I didn't dare look at Ruby. My face burned. I almost jumped up and confessed my guilt, but instead of accusing me, he said, "Mrs. O'Shaughnessy, no one knows horses better than Will. They're gentle as lambs when he's around. He can teach the boy. None better than Will."

I heaved a sigh of relief. I had to calm down. Ruby didn't flinch, but she recognized my panic. Her glare turned my watery backbone to a pillar of ice.

Satisfied, Mom asked Ed, "Does it feel colder up on the ridge? We're somewhat sheltered here in the river valley; we don't get the full wind."

"I think we'll have an early winter. I've never seen so many woolly worms. It'll be a hard one."

Dad shuddered at the mention of wintry weather. I felt sorry for him having to work in the cold every day. His lumbago got worse each year.

"I've lived in Wisconsin all me life," he said. "It's beautiful country and good farmland, too. But it's two suits of long johns too far north if you ask me." He took a bite of his deviled egg, and then held the remainder up for all to see. "Do you think this old devil will warm me up? Ah, well … when I look in the mirror each morning and see myself looking back, I figure the day's off to a good start, even if it is frigid outside; so I'd better enjoy it, 'cause it may be the best one I'll see for a while."

After the meal, we all agreed that the ice cream was the best we'd had in a long time and that the leftover pint should be saved for Sharon and

Ed to eat before he left for home in the morning. Once the table was cleared and the dishes washed, the lovers walked to the river through the evening dusk. Prior experience with Ruby's pranks had convinced Sharon and Ed to stay on the fringes of her territory, even on chilly evenings. They could bundle up against the cold.

Mom, Dad, and we girls played Chinese checkers by the firelight, but Petr turned in early. I couldn't concentrate. I lost the first two games because I failed to develop a line to maneuver, and then I missed other obvious moves. It was time to withdraw to my room. Ruby excused herself and followed me up the stairs, complaining all the while that I was acting too suspicious. I heard Mom say to Dad as they headed up to bed, "Catherine wasn't herself tonight. She must have eaten too much ice cream."

After they had returned from their walk, Sharon and Ed retreated to the side porch swing. Fully clothed in our rooms, Ruby and I heard the chain sing its soprano song and knew it was time.

"You sneak down the back stairs and get the matches," Ruby said. "Bring the whole package so that we can strike them on the box. I'll get the firecrackers and meet you behind the house. But be quiet. Mom and Dad may not be asleep yet."

I eased down the steps while Ruby retrieved the firecrackers. Ten minutes later, we met behind the house. Ruby motioned me to the back corner of the porch, about twenty feet behind where Sharon and Ed swung, oblivious to everything around them. I said, "Hold out the firecrackers, and I'll light them, but throw them straight. Don't hit anyone."

Ruby shook her head. "Oh, no, we'll both throw one. We're in this together."

I may have been reluctant when Ruby proposed the devilment, but I wouldn't be a slacker after I'd agreed. So I stepped back behind the corner of the house, struck a match, and took a firecracker from Ruby's hand. Together, we thrust the fuses into the flame and, when they began to sputter, lobbed the activated mini-bombs behind the unsuspecting lovers.

Ten seconds passed—then BAM! BAM!

Sharon and Ed, who were ascending in the swing at the moment of the explosions, continued their upward flight a full body's length beyond the swing's apogee and sprawled across the porch floor.

A moment later we heard a shotgun blast, and Petr hollered out the window, "Take that you bastards!"

We'd forgotten that he was prone to nightmares and that loud blasts might trigger his war memories.

When the shotgun exploded, Ed jumped up and ran off the porch hollering, "I'll stop them, Sharon." He ran forward and was in full stride when he encountered a frozen depression at the yard's edge. His feet slid out from under him, and his body joined the flight.

Although our ears rang from the explosions, Ruby and I doubled over in laughter when we heard Ed's brave call and the splash as he crashed through the ice. We laughed so hard that we barely made it up the back stairs. It was our good fortune that, at that moment, Dad, Mom, and Petr were racing down the front stairs.

Ruby and I quickly changed into our night clothes and mussed our hair to look like it had been slept on, then we descended the front stairs to ask about the noise.

Because of the darkness, no one noticed the residue on the porch, and all assumed that someone had been shooting close by. Petr apologized profusely.

Ruby, with a straight face, said, "It must have been that Pickle McGraw. I hear he's caused all kinds of ruckus shootin' raccoons at night. They say he's a pistol. He must spend all his time huntin' and causin' a rumpus."

We all agreed that it was probably that rascal McGraw boy hunting raccoon, and then we retreated to our beds. All, that is, except Ruby and me. Ruby had other ideas.

After we'd returned to our room, and I began to get into bed, Ruby said, "Wouldn't you like a little more ice cream before we turn in?"

"Steal Sharon and Ed's ice cream? We all agreed they'd get it tomorrow. You did, too, Ruby."

"I had my fingers crossed," Ruby said. "Besides, we won't take much, just a teaspoon each. They'll never know."

"Haven't we done enough for one night?"

"Not quite. I'm hungry for another spoonful of vanilla. Come on, you might as well join me. You can't tell anyone. You're already up to your neck in crime."

I glared at her.

She frowned back. "Well, maybe not quite that far, but up to your wrists, at least."

Ruby headed quietly down the stairs one more time, and I followed like an obedient puppy. She crept through the back hall, stopping only to retrieve two teaspoons, and into the cold back room where the ice cream was secreted away—and I was right behind her.

"You listen at the door, and I'll find the ice cream." Ruby handed me a spoon. "When I get it open, you bring your spoon, and we'll have another bite."

"Okay, but only one spoonful. We've done enough damage for one night."

"It's a bit late for remorse, especially since you were laughing as hard as I was. It sure is dark in here. I can't see a thing."

Minutes that felt like hours passed as I listened to Ruby moving inside the room. Although Ruby's steps were soft, they sounded stentorian to me because I was so nervous. I just knew someone would hear us.

After a few minutes, Ruby whispered, "I've found it. Come on in but be careful."

When I got close, Ruby reached out and found my hand. She pulled me toward her. "Hand me your spoon; I'll fill it. Then I'll fill mine."

I took the spoonful from Ruby and started back across the room. I was halfway to the door when I decided to stop and eat the ice cream right there, rather than chance spilling it in the dark. By then Ruby had filled her spoon, and together, we slurped the day's last bite of cold vanilla delight.

Except, it wasn't ice cream. By mistake, in the dark, Ruby had dipped into a container of soft lard, and you never saw such fervent gagging and spitting as we staggered from the room toward the sink and water.

7

DANGER ON THE BLUFF

Author's Note

Mother wrote about rattlesnakes on the bluff she so loved to visit. "Rattlesnakes could be a serious problem. I read today that few, if any, people ever get killed by a rattlesnake, but back then they did. Our neighbor, Mr. Temby, had a fourteen-year-old son who was bitten by a rattlesnake. They had to drive him by horse and sled thirteen miles to a doctor in Highland, and he died before they could get there.

"The man who sold us the farm gave us Teddy. He was moving to town and said old Teddy would never be happy away from the farm. Teddy was black and white with long hair, supposedly a border collie. He took to our family immediately. He was an excellent cow dog and also would kill rattlesnakes. The man who gave him to us told about a rattlesnake den up on the bluff on the south edge of our land. He said if we went up on the bluff to get cows or to pick berries that we should take Teddy with us, because he would protect us from rattlesnakes. He was right. One day, while Mother was picking berries up there, Teddy killed a rattlesnake that was coiled and just ready to strike her. He would grab them in the middle and shake them until they died. Another time, when Alice and I, and the Falk kids were walking along the railroad tracks, he grabbed one and shook it to death."

Mother usually bent to Alice's commands, but sometimes Mother rebelled.

I'll tell you about the day when Catherine objected to Ruby's unwillingness to take their neighbor boys, Junkie and Jinks Jenkins, berry picking on the bluff. Ruby finally agreed, but she said they were Catherine's responsibility. On this day, defying Ruby led Catherine to trouble and misery.

The sun rose in the East, burning off the morning dew; not a cloud in the sky. It was sure to be a beautiful day, a day that launched the worst week of my young life.

I started the day full of confidence. Ruby and I had been filling the barn with second crop hay and were exhausted. The sun's heat drained body and soul when working the fields or pitching hay in the loft. Dad said that God won't give you more than you can handle, so I figured He knew what He was doing when He ripened the berries about the time we were too exhausted to throw another forkful.

Time spent in the shade of the high bluff's trees became a welcome reprieve. Thorn cuts were unavoidable, but that was a small price to pay for being alone with my thoughts while I freed nubile berries from their cradles. And before the day was over, the sweet blue juices would stain my lips and streak my chin. It was easy to forget that danger lurked in this Eden.

But even when the bluff wasn't full of sweet, juicy berries, it was my favorite place on the farm. When the weather was good and I had free time, I'd grab an Emily Dickinson anthology, climb up the hill with Teddy, and scan the far-off horizon while pondering my future and reading my favorite poet.

Berries were ripe on the bluff, so Ruby and I had planned for this day all week. Mother warned about snakes and reminded us to take Teddy, but I'd already called him into the house when I saw him begin to follow Petr to the field.

When I stepped into the yard, I saw Ruby facing the neighbor boys, eleven-year-old Junkie and nine-year-old Jinks Jenkins, who sometimes went berry picking with us. They stood, feet planted in our yard's sparse grass, glaring at Ruby.

"No, you can't go blackberry picking today," Ruby said. "Last summer you caused more trouble than you were worth."

"But your mother said we could come," Junkie said. "We don't have any blackberry patches on our land."

"I know that, and I'd like to help," Ruby said, "but last time you almost fell off the bluff. I don't want the responsibility."

"It's like a castle up there," Jinks said. "There's no place so good to play Prince Valiant."

"But we're not going there to play." Ruby's face reddened with each word. "We're going to pick blackberries. If we don't get them soon, the birds will finish them off."

Without thinking, I jumped into the fray, "Do you promise that you'll pick berries?"

"Oh, yes, Catherine," Junkie said. "We brought our pails." He pointed toward two rusted and dented pails that lay on the ground. "We told Mama that we'd bring these buckets home full. She needs them for winter."

I knew that it wouldn't take many berries to fill those small pails, and I felt sorry for the Jenkins family. I took Ruby's arm and drew her aside. "Ruby, you know Mom told Mrs. Jenkins the boys could go. They have all those kids, and their father's laid up. They hardly ever get fresh fruit."

Ruby glared at me. "I'll not take them up there," she said. "I don't want the responsibility."

I stiffened my spine and stood up to Ruby. "Mom wants us to help them." I stamped my foot on the ground and glared right back at my pigheaded sister. "I'll take the responsibility."

Ruby shrugged her shoulders and turned to the boys. "Your pails will be filled long before we're ready to come home. If you come, you'll have to stay and help us fill our buckets."

"But that's not fair," Junkie said. "We'll be picking your berries."

"It wouldn't be fair," I said. "How about they keep half of all they pick."

Ruby turned to Junkie. "You'll do that?"

"If we have to," Jinks said.

Junkie kicked a pail.

"After all, they're our berries," Ruby said.

I grabbed two large pails and called Teddy. "That's fair. Let's take them along."

Ruby glared at me again. "Okay, have it your way. But they're your responsibility. You'll have to watch them. I won't."

We crossed the road and the train tracks and walked to the base of the bluff. Teddy raced back and forth exploring each bush and tree within twenty yards of the trail. When we approached the narrow path that threaded up the hill, a rabbit bolted, and our dog raced after it. Within five minutes he rejoined us, apparently satisfied that he'd protected his charges.

At first, the going was hot as the sun's rays flooded through the scattered branches, but as we got higher, a breeze cooled us, and fifteen minutes later, now at the top and under a canopy of trees, I felt quite comfortable.

Berry bushes grew thick atop the bluff, but we'd have to dig deep to find the biggest berries as the birds had stripped the bushes clean around the edges.

"I know where the big berries are," Jinks said as he and his brother ran ahead through the bushes, thorns slashing red marks across their arms.

Ruby and I took our time. We carefully separated the younger plants to reach the mature, productive bushes with their plump fruit. I knew there would be more berries than we could possibly pick. Last year at this time, we canned a hundred quarts of fresh, juicy blackberries, the product of several long days on the bluff.

But Mother had helped, and I was sure that no one could pick berries as fast as Mother. No matter how hard we tried, no matter how fast we moved our fingers, Ruby, Sharon, and I could never collect as many in a day's picking. Mother didn't hurry, but she picked the largest fruit and never knocked berries off the plant in a rush to fill a pail. "Haste makes waste," she'd say, but Ruby and I never learned that lesson. Mostly though, she didn't fritter time away eating the sweet, juicy fruit like we did.

We'd picked less than an hour when Junkie shouted, "Our pails are full. Can we go home now?"

"Oh, no," Ruby said. "Remember the deal was that you'd help us after you filled your buckets. So get helping."

"I'm hot," Jinks said.

Junkie nodded. "I'm tired."

But when Ruby flashed them an evil look, they wandered toward us as we continued our picking.

Junkie dropped a few berries into her pail before Ruby stopped and glared. "This isn't working," she said as she twisted towards him. "You're knocking more on the ground than you're picking."

I was having the same problem with Jinks, but I hadn't wanted to complain.

"You said you'd help, so get started," Ruby said. "Stop being a hindrance."

I pointed toward my extra pail on the ground. "Instead of throwing berries into our pails, why don't we give them my empty pail so they can find bushes of their own?"

It seemed a good way to keep Junkie away from Ruby.

The boys grabbed the empty pail and wandered away while Ruby and I picked our way through the thickest berries. After a while, Ruby and I were so deep in the bushes that I couldn't see the boys, but because I still heard voices, I knew they couldn't be far away. I didn't see Teddy either, but assumed he was with the boys.

The sun, high in the sky now, burned dew off the leaves, grass, and rocks. My mind on picking, I forgot the boys until I heard Teddy's snarl, followed by a scream and a shout, "We bin bit!"

I dropped my bucket and ran through the bushes toward the shout. At first, all I saw was an upside-down pail. I had warned the boys at other times that there were snakes up here, but I couldn't remember if I reminded them today. My heart beat fast. What I did remember was Ruby's admonition that the boys were my responsibility. I spun around, searching for them.

The bushes were thick, so I stood on tiptoe to look through the foliage, but I didn't see anyone at first. My heart beat so loud that I could feel it thumping against my chest. Then when I looked toward the rock outcroppings at the bluff's edge, my worst fears were realized. Junkie slumped against a rock, his face as white as freshly fallen snow. A dead rattlesnake lay at his feet. Jinks was bent over sobbing, holding his right forearm with his left hand, both drawn tight to his chest. Teddy patrolled their perimeter like a sentry looking for trouble.

Ruby ran up beside me. "Cathy, run faster than you've ever run before and get whoever's at the house, but call Dr. Snyder first. I'll do what I can for the boys, but bring the toboggan up. You'll need help. We've gotta get them down to Dr. Snyder."

I ran until my lungs hurt. I stumbled and fell, but I picked myself up and ran again. I felt the branches whip across my body, but I didn't stop. My arms were bloodied by the brambles, but I hardly noticed. All I could think was that it was my fault. I'd promised Ruby I'd watch them. What if they died? Elmer Chandler died from a snakebite last spring. Now it was the Jenkins boys, and it was my fault. The thought spurred me on. They were my responsibility.

When I got to the house, I found Dad in the yard, but I was so exhausted I couldn't speak. I panted for air as he bent over me. "Snakes," was all I could say. I tried to calm myself and took several deep breaths before I gasped, "Snakes bit the boys. Call the doctor."

Dad didn't ask for details. He ran to the house. Still bent from fatigue, I rushed to the shed where the toboggan hung on the wall. Petr, who must have seen the commotion from the field, raced toward me. By the time he got there, I caught my breath enough to tell him what happened. He lifted the toboggan, and I followed him out of the shed.

Petr and I were across the road when Dad, his arms loaded with blankets, caught us. "Dr. Snyder's on his way," he said. "He'll be here by the time we get the boys down. If we're not back by the time he arrives, Sharon will bring him to meet us."

We ran upward. I struggled to keep up, but nobody waited. I knew they had to get there as fast as possible. At the top, Petr ran toward where I pointed, pulling the toboggan after him.

Dad and I arrived at the scene a few moments after Petr did. Junkie sat like a white marble statue, but Jinks lay on the ground. His body shook, and he didn't seem to hear Ruby's exhortations to stay calm and to breathe deeply. His eyes stared skyward, and except for his shaking, I wouldn't know if he were alive or dead. *Dear God, make him live, please make him live.* It's my fault. I should have kept them close. I should have listened to Ruby and made them stay home. But wishing wouldn't help. We had to get the boys down the hill, to Dr. Snyder.

Ruby and Petr lifted Jinks and placed him on the sled. Even though the day was hot, Dad covered him with blankets. They eased Junkie onto the foot of the toboggan, and although he didn't resist, he didn't utter a word. Ruby grabbed the remaining blankets and wrapped them around him. I cried, too exhausted and upset to help. Ruby anchored the toboggan while the men guided it down the hill. I followed close behind.

As we approached the farm, I could see Dr. Snyder's Model A pulling into the yard and saw him talk to Sharon a moment before he grabbed his bag and ran in our direction. The doctor wasn't a young man, but he ran surprisingly fast and reached us before we crossed the road. He quickly examined Junkie and then turned to Jinks. He looked up at Dad. "We've got to get this boy to the hospital. Get my car over here as fast as you can. I'll care for him while you drive."

Then I heard those dreaded words. "Hurry, Will. It may already be too late."

When Junkie recovered from shock, he told us how the rattlesnake had struck at him after another bit Jinks, but in an instant Teddy had grabbed the serpent in the middle and shook it so hard that he broke its back. Dr. Snyder's examinations confirmed the story: Junkie's pant leg was pierced, and there was dried venom on his skin: evidently Teddy had acted before the snake's fangs penetrated Junkie's flesh.

"Teddy's a hero," Dad said. "That dog deserves steaks for a week."

Jinks hadn't been so lucky. He slipped into a coma on the way to the hospital. Five days passed, but he didn't improve. Dr. Snyder called and said that poison ravaged his system. It'd be touch and go, but because he was young and strong, he might survive. We prayed every night.

The boys had made the mistake of climbing over the rocks on a hot summer morning and disturbing rattlesnakes that were basking in the warmth of the morning sun. Everyone said that it wasn't my fault, but I felt responsible just the same. After all, Ruby said the boys were my duty. And I agreed.

I moped around the farm doing my chores. I sought comfort from Mother, who gladly gave it, but the more solace I received, the more guilt I felt. Jinks had to get better. I couldn't live with myself if he died.

Finally Mother said, "Catherine, you need to get your mind off Jinks for a while. Why don't you go to town and spend the day with Jenny Witherspoon? She's always bright and cheerful. It'll do you good."

I saddled Fanny Too and meandered toward town. I liked Jenny, and I knew Mom was trying to help, but I wasn't in the mood. I rode a while, but eventually stopped, dismounted, and sat under a large burr oak half a mile away from home. Fanny Too grazed in the abundant sweet clover alongside the road.

I languished alone with my thoughts. Finally I knew what I must do. I wanted to go back to the bluff. I hadn't gone there since they brought Jinks down. Until now, I was certain I'd be too afraid to climb the bluff ever again. But now I knew that I must go back. No rattlesnake or dreadful memory would keep me away from my favorite place in the entire world—throne on high, my goddess's lookout.

I remounted Fanny Too, who initially resisted my urging, but eventually, after a wistful look back at the clover, she obeyed the rein. Fanny Too apparently had no weighty problems on her mind—nothing to ponder, no guilt, no regrets—except for leaving that tasty meal.

I was careful not to show myself as I rode past the farm. When I got to the bluff, I dismounted and led Fanny Too part way up the hill. Then I tethered her with a long lead in an open patch of timothy. It was the best I could find, and Fanny Too didn't protest but lowered her head and munched the grass, apparently as satisfied with the timothy as she had been with the clover.

I walked slowly up the hill, eager but apprehensive, too. The memories of five days earlier returned with a vengeance: Jinks lying prone, motionless on the ground; my frantic run for the toboggan; and most horrifying of all, Dr. Snyder saying, "Hurry, Will. It may already be too late."

I glanced about for snakes when I approached the top. Not seeing any movement, I continued to my favorite spot, the big boulder that overlooked my farm below. I never saw vipers at this huge rock. It wasn't full of crevices, and it wasn't an outcropping buried in the hill like the other rock formations on the bluff. It looked as if it'd been placed there by the god Zeus for my pleasure and enlightenment.

I saw no movement below—no one in the house yard, no one in the barnyard, no one in the bean field behind the barn. I surveyed the beans, a strange crop for the Wisconsin River valley. They covered the earth with a deep green blanket that was now turning golden. Dad said that beans and alfalfa were good feed for the cattle and much better for the soil than corn or oats, and someday people would discover lots of commercial uses for beans. But unfortunately it seemed that day would be too far in the future to help my dad.

Suddenly someone came from the house. I looked carefully and saw that it was Sharon with a pan of dishwater that she emptied over the fence into the pasture. If we had hogs, they'd clean up the refuse as fast as it was dumped, but Dad wouldn't have hogs. I wasn't sure why, but I was glad. I didn't like hogs. I didn't like their snorts. I didn't like their rutting, their tearing up the ground. But most of all, I didn't like their smell. Nothing smelled as bad as a hog pen. I liked cows when they were out in the pasture. And I liked chickens and sheep, but we didn't keep many sheep. Dad said they ate the grass to its roots, killing some of it, and leaving little for his cows. And that wasn't good. After all, the cow is queen on a dairy farm.

I saw Dad and Petr leave the barn and head for the wagon, soon to straighten its hitch and pull it to an open area. I knew they'd now go to the barn and return with a pair of horses. Maybe they'd go to the field to bring back a load of corn for the silo.

I looked toward the river and saw our cows grazing slowly across the pasture, moving as if they had no worries in the world. We had one Black Angus, too. I didn't like to think about its fate, nor did I like beef on my dinner plate. I'd rather eat veggies and fruit and no meat at all. Well, maybe ham and bacon if I could keep my mind off the hog's filthy, smelly pens.

Birds fluttered through the trees and sang their joyful melodies. If only I didn't have this awful millstone around my neck, I'd join them in song. The sun filtered through the leaves to brighten the rocks around me, but I shivered just the same, and tears ran down my cheeks. The heavens took pity, and from a single cloud, raindrops gently washed my tears away.

A rivulet ran down the bluff. If the tree line wasn't so thick, I'd be able to see over the fields to the river. I thought of all the places that water could go, and I was envious. It could flow from the Wisconsin to the Mississippi, and then south to New Orleans. Maybe someday I'd go to New Orleans, or "Orlans" as my cousin Gusta called it. Gusta told me all about Orlans, and it sounded like a terribly wicked place. I giggled to myself. Wicked, just like Gusta. Maybe someday I'd be a wicked woman, too. I blushed thinking about it.

I wondered where the water went after it left the Gulf. There were so many possibilities. Would it go around the Cape of Good Hope into the Atlantic, or might it flow around Baja California into the Pacific? Why, the water that ran past my farm could go anywhere in the world. Isn't that amazing! Anywhere in the world! Maybe someday I could go anywhere, too. I wished I could get into my rowboat and float—to Rio, to London, to Hong Kong. Anyplace exotic would do—anyplace beyond my worry for Jinks.

Or maybe, like Emily Dickinson, I should live a life of seclusion. Life would be less painful that way. The thoughts brought a favorite Dickinson poem to mind.

A drop fell on the apple tree
Another on the roof;
A half a dozen kissed the eaves,
And made the gables laugh.

A few went out to help the brook,
That went to help the sea.
Myself conjectured, Were they pearls,
What necklaces could be!

The dust replaced in hoisted roads
The birds jocoser sung;
The sunshine threw his hat away,
The orchards spangles hung.

The breezes brought dejected
And bathed them in the glee;
The East put out a single flag,
And signed the fete away.

I thought about how Ruby had stayed atop the bluff, all alone, to care for Junkie and Jinks when she didn't know whether they'd live or die. They could have died right there in her arms. How romantic it'd be if it were a story in a book, but this was no story. It was life and death here on the river. I admired Ruby so—her courage, her decisiveness, her spunkiness—a spunkiness that I knew I could never match. I hoped I'd be near Ruby for the rest of my life. I hoped that I'd die first. I didn't want to think about life without Ruby.

The sun dropped behind the trees, and a breeze blew across the bluff. I shivered. I hadn't brought a jacket, and it was too warm for a chill, but it wasn't the breeze that coaxed the tremor from deep inside my soul. However hard I tried, I couldn't stop thinking about Jinks. I'd never really liked him, and that thought made me feel guiltier than ever.

I knew I'd have to return home soon. The sun had fallen out of sight, and dusk was setting in. I didn't want to walk down that hill in the dark. Suddenly I remembered Fanny Too. I'd completely forgotten her, so engulfed was I in self-pity and guilt. Fanny Too hadn't had water all day long. How could I have been so uncaring?

I rushed down the hill to where my horse was tethered, but Fanny Too was nowhere in sight. I called and looked around, but no Fanny Too. I ran toward home as fast as my legs would go, hoping that Fanny Too had made her way back. The run reminded me of my recent dash down the hill, and I shivered violently once again. Now past the thinning brush at the bottom, I looked toward home.

Ruby rushed toward me. "Where have you been all day? Mom and Dad are frantic. Fanny Too came home hours ago. Mom called Jenny's house, but she said you hadn't been there." Ruby grabbed my shoulder and pushed me towards the farmstead. "Hurry, get home and relieve Mom's worry. You've been moping around so much lately that Sharon thought you went and jumped in the river. Dad and Petr rode down to look. How could you have caused so much trouble, sis?"

I fumbled for words, but before I could answer, Ruby said, "Oh, by the way, Dr. Snyder called. Jinks came out of his coma. He's going to be okay."

I stopped and turned toward Ruby, feeling numb as though in a trance. Then I slipped to the cool ground, and tears gushed down my face.

UNFETTERED AND FREE

8

BANISHED TO WISCONSIN

Author's Note
Mother never told about the incident that led to Gusta being sent north. She knew that Gusta's mother thought Gusta to be incorrigible, completely lacking self-discipline. Mother said she got some discipline after she came to live with them. But it wasn't easy. Gusta was worldly and resourceful, and she didn't readily bend to anyone's wishes.

My story describes a cousin who lives on the edge of danger, and I imagine an evening of events that led to Gusta's exile to the Wisconsin farm. (I kept Gusta's real-life name in my stories.)

Ruby heard Mom tell Dad that cousin Gusta was being sent to live with us. She might as well have been banished to Siberia. Gusta hated cold weather. I knew that British criminals were banished to far-off Australia. What terrible crime could cousin Gusta have committed? She told us her story soon after she arrived.

"Gusta, is that you?" her mother called from the kitchen.

She must have heard Gusta slip in the back door. There was no easy out now. "Yes, Mother. I stopped at Marjorie's on the way home. She wasn't at school today, and I wanted to see if she was ill or something."

"Oh … wasn't today your dress rehearsal? Doesn't she play Juliet? She must have been awfully sick to have missed that."

"She was. She's really sick. Her mother wouldn't let me in the house. I had to talk through the window."

"I suppose you know your part quite well after practicing all day, don't you?"

"Of course, but I've only got two lines—thank heavens. I wish we'd do something modern—maybe … 'The Children's Hour.'"

"Gusta, that's naughty. It was banned in Boston."

"I know. We'd raise some eyebrows, wouldn't we? Course, Spears would never do it. The Neanderthal."

"So your practice went well? Funny thing, Mr. Spears called and asked if you were ill, said you weren't in school today. I suppose he didn't recognize you in your costume."

"Must not have."

"Gusta, this has to stop. It's the second time he's called this month. It's time you got discipline. Maybe a boarding school. You can't run vadon."

"Mom, talk English."

"Vadon? You are wild. You'd better learn some Hungarian … and soon. I got a letter from Marguerite today. I'm thinking about bringing her to live with us. She's worried sick about that madman, Hitler, worried that the White Terror will come back to Hungary."

Oh, great, Aunt Marguerite with them, now. And she'd thought her mother's old country morality suffocated her. "Mom, don't even think about it." A boarding school?

Her mother had set new rules after the missed play practice, but Gusta'd not heard more about Aunt Marguerite. Maybe she wouldn't come after all.

"Gusta, did you see that handsome fellow who just came in the gym?" Marjorie said.

Gusta jerked her head around. "Oh, my God, I'll just die if he asks me to dance."

"You'll die all right—your mother'll kill you. I heard her warn, no older guys, and didn't you say she expected you home by ten o'clock."

Marjorie grabbed Gusta's arm, but Gusta pulled away. "He's at least twenty-five," Marjorie said. "It's that Mason guy. His daddy owns the biggest ranch in Chester County. What's he doing over here?"

Gusta said, "He's coming this way."

Marjorie turned red. "Right toward us, and he's got his eye on you, Gusta." She eased her way toward Gil who stood on the sidelines with the other freshman class boys who took turns pushing each other into couples who'd danced too close.

"Hello, Miss. I'm Billy Bob Mason. I couldn't help but notice you. There's not a more elegant woman on the floor tonight. Why, you stand out like a rose among the thorns. Would you do me the honor?"

"Mr. Mason, I do declare. You are a gentleman. I'd love to dance. It's a Texas two-step, my favorite."

Billy Bob held out his hand, and Gusta followed him onto the dance floor. "Don't you just love this band?" Gusta said. "The Texas Playboys, and they call it Texas swing. They're the best we've ever had here in Winsum. I must tell the leader. Do you know his name?"

"I heard someone say Bob. I'd remember that, wouldn't I? Wills, I think."

They danced the set. Gusta flashed a smug smile each time she passed her classmates. Billy Bob, intent on her cleavage, never looked up.

When the music stopped, Gusta led Billy Bob to the stage. He never raised his eyes. "Mr. Wills, is it?"

"Bob Wills. Your name?"

"Gusta, Gusta Tregonning."

"Tregonning? That's not a Texas name. I've not heard it before."

"It's Cornish. My father's grandparents came from Cornwall. Miners, most of them, I guess. He's gone, died when I was a baby. I just love your music, Mr. Wills."

"Well, thank you, Miss Gusta. I must say, you're the most striking young lady here tonight, and you dance like Ginger Rogers."

Gusta blushed. "You're too kind. I do hope that I get to hear you again sometime, Mr. Wills. I'd go a long way to dance to your music."

"Well, thank you again. We'll make that a date. I'll try to book near here."

Ten o'clock came and passed. Marjorie finally caught Gusta's eye and motioned her to the side. "Daddy's waited a half hour. Let's get going."

"You go ahead. Billy Bob said he'd drive me home. Would you call

Mother and tell her that I just had to hear The Texas Playboys to the end? They're the best ever."

"Sure, you want me to face her. She'll be furious."

"She'll get over it. Go on now."

By eleven o'clock, when the music stopped, Billy Bob had seldom raised his eyes.

Gusta led Billy Bob past the stage on their way from the gym. "Mr. Wills, thank you so much. I just love your swing music."

"See you next time, Gusta. I'll get back. That's a promise."

She rushed Billy Bob toward the door. "Better get hustling. Gotta pay the piper."

Billy Bob sped down the highway in his Ford Phaeton convertible. Gusta leaned back and took her cigarettes out. "Have a smoke, Billy Bob."

He waved her off and stepped down on the accelerator.

"Better slow down, Billy Bob. I see cops along this road most every time I drive it."

"My pa owns the cops in West Texas." He sped on, but slowed and turned down the dirt road when he got to Smith's crossing.

"Billy Bob, take me straight home. I'm in trouble already."

He reached for Gusta's hand and then drove another hundred yards before pulling into an abandoned drive.

She pulled her hand away and slid toward the door. "You better not have ideas, Billy Bob. I'm not that kinda girl. Get me home—now!"

"I been eyeing your breasts all night, Gusta," Billy Bob said as he slid toward her, "and now I'm going to see what they're made of—for a starter."

He grabbed at Gusta's blouse, but she slapped his hand away. He slid hard against her, pinning her against the door with his right arm while he slipped his left hand into her cleavage. Quick as a skittish West Texas deer, Gusta pulled a pen knife from her purse and jabbed it deep into Billy Bob's arm.

"You bitch, you," he screamed as he jerked away and grabbed his blood-soaked limb.

Gusta jumped from the car and ran back the way they'd come. She heard the roar of the engine, and she ran faster, but the car never slowed as it weaved past her. She saw blood running down the door panel, and Billy Bob screamed as he flew past, "You'll pay for this, Gusta Tregonning."

Why did trouble always find her, she wondered as she walked back toward the paved road. The new moon barely lighted her way as she walked along the blacktop highway. Maybe she'd get lucky, and a car'd come along, but not likely this time of night. Snakes—she had to watch for snakes and other vermin attracted to the warm pavement as the night air cooled the ground. She walked slowly, straining to see the road ahead. What would Billie Bob do?

She'd walked a mile or two; then she heard it. The sound of a million dry leaves protesting their demise. Her foot stopped in midair. She knew she couldn't take another step until she'd located the source of that death chant. She felt that her eyes would pop from their sockets as she peered into the darkness. She thought that it was ahead and to her left, probably on the road, but she didn't dare step into the tall grass next to the narrow shoulder. She'd weakened from the tension when she heard a car in the distance and saw lights shining over the hill behind her. Thank heavens, relief. She'd only have to hold her pose a little longer.

The car's headlights illuminated her and the rattlesnake as it slithered away into the tall grass. Thank you, God, she thought as the car slowed down. Then, red and blue flashing lights blinded her. She'd expressed her gratitude too soon.

"Are you Gusta? Gusta Tregonning?" the officer called as he stepped from his car.

"Yes, Officer," Gusta squeaked.

"I have a warrant for your arrest. You'll have to come to the station with me." He opened the back door, the door behind the screen. "Get in."

"But why, Officer?" She knew the answer.

"We'll talk about it at the station house, young lady."

The officer pointed to a chair. "Sit down, Miss Gusta. You could be in deep do-do for what you did. That's Seth Mason's boy. His daddy casts a long shadow. He'd have my job if he lived in this county and I didn't book you."

"Is Billy Bob okay? Will I go to jail?"

"He'll be fine—just needed a few stitches. "I've got a good idea what happened, but you can't be stabbing every Romeo who takes you home. You need to be more careful about your companions, young lady."

"I was just defending my honor, sir."

"Yes, but I'll have to confiscate that weapon. Next time, you might not be so lucky."

Gusta opened her purse and took the knife out.

The officer reached for it. "I'll take that."

"I sure wish you didn't have to. It was my daddy's."

"I knew Nicholas. It was the arsenic, I think, used lots in the mining. A good man. No one messed with him, I'll tell you."

"I sure wish I'd gotten to know him. I was only a year when he—"

"Far too young." He reached out for the knife. "Your daddy's knife?"

"Daddy left it with other keepsakes in his treasure box. Told Mom to give them to me. I'm ashamed that I dishonored him."

"Well, I can't take your daddy's treasures, but do me a favor. Put it away. Next time, I can't ignore the weapon." He walked to his desk and picked up the phone. "I'll call your mother."

Now the real trouble'd begin, Gusta knew.

"Gusta, your mother's sending her hired man, Chester, to pick you up. You'd better prepare yourself. She's not a happy woman."

When she arrived home, her mother was furious. "Gusta Tregonning, this is the last straw. You're an incorrigible tramp. You need to get discipline, and I know just where to send you. Chester has agreed to run the ranch for a while. I'm going to Hungary to help my sister get her affairs in order. She's coming here to stay, and you're going away."

9

WHATEVER WERE THEY DOING IN THE BACK ROOM?

Author's Note

Knowing that she loved music and dancing, the O'Shaughnessy's held a house dance to welcome Gusta to Wisconsin (*Bittersweet Harvest*).

Mother had written in *From High on the Bluff*, "Gusta knew more about the birds and bees than I did at forty. She also smoked, but never in the house." Although Mother said that real-life Gusta wasn't thought to be promiscuous, after Gusta took Sharon's beau, Ed, into the back room in my fictitious account, Catherine wasn't so sure.

All my family loved music and dancing, and we often rolled back the carpet to square dance. Dad called the squares, and we danced until we dropped from exhaustion. Those were happy times—until that night we held a "Welcome to Wisconsin" dance for Gusta.

All our neighbors were there. Dad, Hank Swenson, and Clooney McBride played music, and Dad also called the squares.

Honor your partner, honor your corner.

Gusta created a bit of a ruckus when she made a grand entrance dressed like Jean Harlow, but it didn't spoil the fun I had dancing—I loved to dance—and it was a grand night for everyone.

All face your partner, do-sa-do, back to back around you go.

But I couldn't believe my eyes when Gusta grabbed Ed Meadow's hand and led him toward the back porch. Sharon's boyfriend, faithful old Ed, went to the back porch with Gusta. Men—they just can't be trusted.

I knew that I shouldn't intrude, but I just couldn't help myself, so I followed, but I slowed so that I wouldn't disrupt their plans. I felt like Sherlock Holmes stalking two criminals. As I eased toward the porch, I heard and saw the quick flare-up of a kitchen match.

All promenade, two by two.

"Do you smoke cigarettes, Ed?"

"Oh, no, Gusta, but I smoked a pipe once. I thought it smelled good, but it didn't taste so good."

"You don't smoke because it tastes good, silly."

"Then why do it, if it doesn't taste good?"

"There're lotsa things you do that don't taste good," Gusta said, giggling.

Ed looked confused.

"I'll light a Chesterfield for you."

She took a package of cigarettes from her purse and placed one between her lips, and then sucked through it from the nearly extinguished match. Then she placed the lit cigarette between Ed's lips and put a second one in her mouth, before standing on tiptoe and leaning in as if for a kiss.

Ed jumped back.

"Ed, do you think I'm going to assault you? I just want a light."

She leaned toward him again, touching the end of her cigarette to the end of his.

I felt dizzy.

Ed looked dizzy, too.

"I think I'd better go back. Sharon will—"

"Ed, you've got to learn the two-step. I can't dance it alone. Just puff on that cigarette. It'll calm you."

Ed leaned back against the railing, but I didn't think he looked calm. He looked a bit green.

Oats all heated, spuds all froze
Wheat crops busted, wind still blows
Looks some gloomy, I'll admit
Get up Dobbin—we ain't through yit

"Okay, Ed, let's try it."

"What?"

"The dance, Ed. The two-step."

"Oh, yeah. Let's try it."

Ed staggered a bit as he approached Gusta. "What do I do?"

"First of all, relax."

Ed slumped.

"I didn't say fall over. I said relax. Stand in front of me."

Ed took a few steps toward Gusta and stopped, leaving a gap between them.

"Closer," Gusta said, grabbing Ed's arms and yanking him forward, smack into the feathered boa that she'd crossed over her bosom. Ed looked down, right into Gusta's plunging neckline. Then he retreated like a scared rabbit.

"Ed, we can't two-step if you're halfway across the porch. Come here and put your right hand on my waist. I won't bite."

Ed moved forward and reached for Gusta's waist—until the tips of his fingers made contact—and stood stiff.

"Okay, that's a start. Now, raise your right elbow and bend it a little. Take my hand."

Gusta clutched Ed's right hand with a grip that wouldn't allow him to dart away again. "Now, on the beat, step forward quickly with your left foot."

"I don't want to step on you, Miss Gusta."

"Don't worry, Ed. I'll move quicker than you. It's not my feet that I like caressed."

The hussy, I thought.

"On the second beat, step forward with your right foot. Okay, now do it again with your left foot, but slowly this time, then pause on the fourth beat. Now, on the fifth beat, move forward slowly with your right foot, then pause on the sixth beat. Good. Let's practice."

I love wine and Jeanne loves silk
The little pigs love buttermilk
And ever since the world began
The ladies love a ladies man

I watched. Gusta was elegant, so good that she covered Ed's clumsy mistakes. And after fifteen minutes of practice, they looked as if they'd danced together for weeks. I turned and was about to tiptoe away when Gusta called, "Okay, Catherine, you can come out now. What do you think of this naughty duet? Do you think we'll shock everyone with our lewd dance?"

"I … I think you're graceful. Will you teach me, Gusta?"

"Someday, Catherine. I'm afraid I've done enough damage already this night. Take Ed back to the dance. I'll be there as soon as I've finished this Chesterfield."

The wise old owl he lived in oak
The more he heard the less he spoke
The less he spoke the more he heard
Why aren't you like that old bird

Ed no sooner entered the living room than Sharon ran out of the kitchen, a dish towel scrunched in her fist. "Where were you, Ed. I've looked all over."

Ed looked so distraught that I thought he needed some help, so I spoke up. "Gusta was teaching him the two-step—"

"In the back room?"

She threw the dish towel at Ed, turned, and raced back into the kitchen. I didn't have much sympathy for Ed, but I believed in fairness, so I followed. I knew that I should try to persuade Sharon and Mother that Ed did nothing wrong. Mother seemed to accept my defense of Ed, but although she tried to calm Sharon, Sharon wasn't as forgiving. I wasn't so sure about Gusta's intent, but that went unsaid.

If I had a girl who wouldn't dance
I'll tell you what I would do
I'd put that gal in an old row boat
And paddle my own canoe

PUPPET ON A STRING

Ruby slipped away from the dancers and sidled over in my direction. "I heard that Sharon's angry with Ed and Gusta. What happened?"

I explained the back-porch episode, not omitting any detail. After all, Ruby was my friend and confidante. And besides, Ruby admired Gusta. "I explained to Mom, and she tried to calm Sharon down, but I'm not sure it helped much."

"I said life would change when Gusta got here. She sure is a pistol," Ruby said.

"You don't think she has eyes for Ed, do you?" I said.

"Naw, these boys are too tame for her," Ruby said. "Those she dated back in Texas are real cowboys. They're humdingers, wild as the Texas prairie. I think she's just funnin' Ed. Poor Ed's skittish as a cornered bunny."

The squirrels they love a hickory tree
The clover loves the bumblebee
The flies they love molasses and
The ladies love a ladies man

I hadn't noticed that Gusta had slipped from the room until she came down the stairs with her ukulele. She talked to Dad, and he stopped the music.

Gusta waved at her audience. "I'm so pleased to meet y'all that I've decided to return your kindness." She took Dad's hand and smiled toward Mom. "I'm sorry if I embarrassed y'all, but I bought these clothes for a special occasion, and I couldn't think of anything more special than this dance. Tonight is the first I've worn them. Please forgive me."

She was so sincere and so contrite that, at that moment, I didn't think anyone there wouldn't forgive Gusta her worst transgressions. She could charm a doubting Thomas if she put her mind to it.

"I've brought my ukulele to play a song." She signaled toward Dad. "When you're ready, I'll lead. Y'all will know this song."

On, Wisconsin! On, Wisconsin!
Grand old badger state!
We, thy loyal sons and daughters,
Hail thee, good and great.

Soon everyone was singing so loud that the doors rattled in their casings. We'd all forgot that little children were sleeping in the guest bedroom, until the screams began. After the song, Gusta set her ukulele aside and regained everyone's attention.

"Now, I'd like to show you a Texas dance that I hope y'all like. I can't do the dance alone, so with Cousin Sharon's blessing, I'll ask Ed to help." She turned to Sharon. "And I promise." She crossed her heart. "I'll help Ed teach you the dance the second time through. Is that okay, Cousin Sharon?"

Sharon blushed but nodded her agreement, and soon everyone clapped their hands to the beat, none more enthusiastically than my oldest sister.

And when the dance finished, Gusta took Sharon's hand and led her onto the dance floor. With a smile as wide as the living room sofa, Sharon followed her cousin toward Ed.

But no matter how repentant she acted, I knew that for Gusta, tomorrow would be a new day.

All we need to make us happy
Is two little boys to call me pappy
One named Paul and the other named Davey
One loves ham and the other loves gravy

I bumped into Phil Withers as he hurried across the room. I knew that Ruby had a crush on Phil. "Where's your sister?" he said.

I pointed toward the corner of the room. "She's over there talking to Gusta."

Phil rushed over, and I followed. Phil grabbed Ruby's arm. "Come on, Ruby. This is the last dance. You promised."

Gusta stepped forward. "I don't believe I've met your friend, Ruby. Would you be so kind?"

"Oh, sure, Gusta. This is Phil—Phil Withers." She nodded toward Gusta. "My cousin, Gusta."

"Mr. Withers, I didn't know men were so handsome in Wisconsin." As Gusta took Phil's arm and led him onto the dance floor, she turned to Ruby and said, "You don't mind if we dance this one last dance, do you, Ruby? It would be the perfect ending to a perfect evening."

I couldn't help but laugh. Now it was Ruby's turn to fume.

"I hate that Gusta," she said.

Gusta wasn't about to wait for tomorrow to upset my sisters. I couldn't help but wonder if I might be next on her list

I've got a cow I call Old Blue
But all that crazy cow can do
Is shake her horns and beller and moo
So promenade boys two by two

10

GUSTA BREAKS CURFEW

Author's Note

Mother wrote in her book, "Gusta, as we called her, was a beautiful dancer and liked to go to dances. A neighbor had a Victrola and some records like *Tea for Two*, which was very good for doing the two-step, and *Melody of Love*, which was good for a slow waltz. Gusta loved to listen and dance to them. One night she went to a dance with a fellow she knew and didn't get home until three o'clock in the morning. That was very late for our house, clearly violating its rules. Mother was up waiting for her when she arrived home and sat and preached to her for about an hour. Gusta politely listened. She didn't sass, but when Mother got all through, Gusta said, 'Aunt Lizzie, you should have been a preacher.' And she meant it."

After reading Mother's account of how Gusta violated her Aunt Lizzie's rules, I felt compelled to tell the whole story, to include the shocking details.

Gusta's father, in real life, had to defend himself when challenged by mine employees, just as Mary described to Gusta in this story. Although to Mother's knowledge, no one jumped through a car window when dating Gusta, that really happened to Mother on one of her dates, and for the same reason, the dog howled when it's tail got pinched by the door.

Gusta had a nose for mischief, but it seemed like every time she upset someone, she knew exactly how to get back in his or her favor.

Even more surprising was the way Gusta handled Mother and Dad. I've never seen the likes of it. Gusta wrapped Dad around her little finger. Anyone who charmed Dad like that could snatch wool off a nervous sheep. And she was almost as successful with Mother. Ruby and I watched in wonderment. Many a time we wished we had Gusta's daring. I'll never forget the time that Gusta missed curfew by two hours. I was certain that Mother would skin her hide that night.

Gusta was about to go out the door when Mother grabbed her arm. Mother looked like my school's principal when he scolded the boys for smoking behind the school.

"Gusta," Mother said, "I expect you to be home by midnight. That's the rule for my girls. If you're not home by then, you'll be grounded for a month. Do you understand?"

"Yes, Aunt Mary. I'll be home. Don't you worry about me."

"Well, I do worry." She looked towards me and Ruby. "I worry about all my family. Especially you, Gusta, going out in a motor car. Anything can happen, and besides, I think Elmer Hampton is too old for you. Why, he's out of high school."

"But he's the only boy I know with a motor car."

"Do you think he'd give me a ride?" I said.

"Count on it."

"Do you really think so? I've heard he's awfully particular with it, that he never gives rides."

"Don't you worry about that," Gusta said. "He'll be back tomorrow. Just you wait and see. Get your duster and goggles out."

"But—I don't have a duster and goggles."

"I wish I knew what your father would want me to do," Mother said.

"I think he'd want me to be happy. And I am happy here with his family. Why, it's just like home, only better. I have three sisters. I won't disappoint you. I promise, Aunt Mary."

Midnight came and went. Dad paced the floor, and Mother and I were up, too. I knew that Mother and Dad were worried about Gusta, but I thought that Gusta could take care of herself. I couldn't keep my mind off Elmer's motor car.

"Don't worry," Dad said. "She'll be okay. Elmer's a responsible lad. He's got money, but that shouldn't be held against him. He came by it honestly, inherited it from his grandfather."

"Catherine, go back to bed," Mother said. "You can't help here."

"But, Mom, I'm worried, too. What if they wrecked his motor car?"

"None of us will be fit tomorrow if we spend the night pacing the floor," Mother said. "If anything happens, someone will call us. No news is good news, you know."

I headed up the stairs to bed, but at first, I couldn't sleep. And when I finally did, I dreamed about a motor car speeding down the lane. I sat next to Elmer, all decked out in a tight duster and a calotte with its goggles pulled down. Gusta and Ruby rode in the back seat, their faces bare and their hands held over their mouths. They squealed and gagged on the dust that filled the air around them. It was a grand dream that ended abruptly when a dog yelped in pain and, moments later, a motor car roared out of the driveway and down the road. Now fully awake, I heard Gusta shout, "You cowardly Yankee! You're as ungallant and cold as your Northern weather!"

I had no idea what time it was, but when we heard the front door slam shut and footsteps below, Ruby and I slipped from our beds and edged down the stairs. I tried to read the watch that Gusta had given me, but the kitchen light was too dim to illuminate the stairway. I could see Mother's face, and I thought that Gusta was surely in hot water this time.

Gusta stood in the faint lamplight. Her blue velvet dress was covered with mud, the V-neckline was torn, exposing her bra, and the ivory appliqué lace hung by threads.

"What happened?" Mother said. "Are you okay?"

"I'm okay, Aunt Mary, just frazzled. And mad as a cornered rattlesnake. That Elmer is no gentleman. I never want to see him again."

My heart sank. It appeared that I'd lost my chance to ride in a motor car, even if it would have been in the back seat.

"Did he do this to you?" Mother said. "Was he—was he improper?"

"Did Elmer ravage me? I'd kick his knackers into his bladder if he tried. We got stuck in the mud this side of Ferris Crossing, and I tried to push us out, but I hooked my gown on the bumper and slipped into the mire. We were in too deep."

"What were you doing at Ferris Crossing? That's off limits for my girls."

Ferris Crossing was a roadside bar that had a bad reputation. We girls had never been there. I don't even think that Dad had stopped there.

But we'd heard plenty about it. My friends at school whispered they not only sold liquor, but they had rooms upstairs that men visited. But I haven't anything more to say about that.

"We walked back to Abel's bar to get help," Gusta said. "It took four men to push us out, but one Texan could have done it easy. They were so drunk they joshed Elmer about his Lizzie. Said it'd serve us right to walk home, clear our thinking 'bout horses and Lizzies."

"Do you know what time it is, Gusta?"

"I know it's late. I'm sorry. I couldn't help it."

"You shouldn't have let Elmer go so far from home. You were asking for trouble, and now you've got it. You know what I said about being grounded? No more outings for the rest of the month, young lady."

"Aunt Mary!"

"Gusta, you know what the Bible says about honoring your father and mother. Your father's dead, and your mother's asked me to help. I'm responsible for you, so I can't have you disobeying rules. I love you like you're one of my own girls. I must treat you the same."

"Yes, Aunt Mary. I'm sorry."

I nodded in agreement.

Gusta looked contrite, but she always looked contrite when she got into trouble.

Ruby whispered, "She'll learn that Mom means what she says."

"Your father'd turn over in his grave if he knew how undisciplined you are." Mother placed her hand on Gusta's arm. "He was a disciplined man. He'd want me to be firm, to expect you to be responsible. You do want to please him, don't you?"

"But how can I please him? I never knew him. Aunt Mary, please tell me all about him."

Gusta was a wily one. She knew that Mother wanted her to know her father, who died before she was old enough to remember.

"I will sometime, but this is about you, Gusta. It's about you learning responsibility. I didn't say anything the night of the welcoming dance, but you must know that you hurt Ruby when you took that last dance away from her. More than anyone, Ruby looks up to you."

I poked Ruby's side and whispered, "See, Mom looks out for you, too."

Ruby remained silent. I guess she hadn't told Mom that she and Gusta had made up.

"I didn't mean to, Aunt Mary. Please tell me about Daddy. If I knew about him, maybe I could reform."

"Gusta, all right, I'll tell you about Nicholas." Mother sat in a chair. "It was a tragedy he died so young. He was a respected leader. When he was appointed to his first mining superintendency in New Mexico, he was only nineteen years old. The men he governed were older and hardened convicts from the East who were sent to the Western gold mines. Their leader threatened Nick, saying no kid was going to tell him what to do. Nick was a big man, but raw. He told me, '"I never put up such a fight in my life, and I whipped the tar out of him.'"

Gusta sat cross-legged on the floor and stared into Mother's eyes. She looked like an awestruck primary student listening to her teacher read *Alice in Wonderland*.

"You'd think those men would've held a grudge. But you know, when your father left that mine to become superintendent of the largest gold mine in the West, those convicts collected money and gave him a two-karat diamond ring. All gathered to wish him well. Some even cried. That was the kind of man your father was. He earned respect from everyone. He'd want you to do the same, Gusta."

Gusta sighed. "Golly, I never knew. Aunt Mary, you oughta been a preacher. I'll try to be like him. I really will." She rose and took her aunt's hand. "May I go out this weekend? I've just gotta go to the dance at the civic center."

"No, Gusta. I said the month, and I must stick to it."

Ruby and I rushed to our room when Gusta turned toward the stairs. We could see that she was upset.

The next morning at breakfast, Ruby said, "Gusta, what was all that commotion last night?"

"The dog howling?"

"And the car racing down the driveway."

"The big coward. Texas men would never be so ungallant."

"What happened?"

"Well, after the mess at Ferris Crossing—"

"You went to Ferris Crossing?" I said. "Only bad girls go there."

"We didn't go to Ferris Crossing until we needed help."

"What happened?" Ruby said.

"Elmer got stuck in mud, the fool."

"I saw your dress in the tub," I said. "But don't worry; Mom'll fix it."

Gusta nibbled at a piece of Swiss cheese. "I don't care. I've got lots more."

"Did he make you push him out of the mud?" Ruby said.

"He did at first. He insisted that no one else could drive that car, but after I slipped and ripped my dress, he could see I wasn't heavy enough, so he told me to get behind the wheel—but he couldn't push us out either."

"Did he get muddy, too?" Ruby said.

"He sure did, after I pulled the throttle all the way out. You should've seen the mud fly! If I'd have known how cowardly he'd be, I'd have left it out longer. That's when we went to the Crossing for help."

Ruby's eyes got big. I could see by the grimace on her face that Ruby was horrified. I was, too. Ruby was courageous, but she'd never have disobeyed Mother like this.

"What was all the noise we heard?" Ruby said.

"Well, I told him that Aunt Mary would be furious, his bringing me home so late, and that she'd tan his hide."

"She'd not have tanned him," I said, "but she'd have given him a piece of her mind."

"Well, I was mad as a floundering hog already, so I wanted him to be as scared as I was for him getting me home late."

"Ha!" Ruby said. "So?"

"He walked me to the door and wanted a kiss."

"You kissed him?" I said.

"No, silly, I didn't kiss him. I was too mad to kiss him, but I got a whole lot madder real soon."

"What happened?" Ruby said.

"Ruby, does Aunt Mary have more of this Swiss cheese?"

"Well, what happened?"

"When he reached for me, I stepped back and pushed the door open, and Teddy must have been waiting. The door caught his tail. When he howled, Elmer ran."

"You hurt Teddy?" I said.

"He didn't even open the car door. He dived through the window and tore down the driveway. You'd have thought Lucifer was close behind." Gusta bit into a chunk of cheese. "I sure do like this Swiss." She took another bite. "Why, a Texas man would've stayed and explained. He wouldn't have let me take all the heat. That little coward."

After breakfast, I saw Gusta approach Dad before he left the house for the barn and heard her say, "Uncle Will, I'll just die if I can't go to the dance Saturday night, but Aunt Mary said I'm not to leave the house for a whole month." She took his big, burly hand between her small, soft ones. "You know how I love to dance. Can't you do something, Uncle Will?"

"So you want me to be your emissary. Or is it your attorney?" Dad slowly shook his head and smiled down on her. "My dear, you're a manipulator, now aren't you? But a charming one, I must admit. I'll see what I can do."

I could see that Gusta had Dad wrapped around her little finger.

Dad must have said the right thing to Mother because that Saturday, Mother let Gusta go with Ruby and me to the town dance. But Mother laid down the law. "Don't you dare come home with anyone but Ruby and Catherine. You come when they come. Do you understand, Gusta?"

"Yes, Aunt Mary. I'll do exactly as you say."

11

GUSTA BAMBOOZLES THE BOYS

Author's Note

Catherine was influenced evermore by Gusta and her exploits during the year she lived with them. She was envious of Gusta's wealth, enamored by her skill on the dance floor, shaken by her loose talk, and shocked by her swearing, smoking, and casual talk of sex. But she never expected and wasn't prepared for the day that Gusta led her to a dalliance with three sleazy boys.

I didn't believe Sharon when she called Gusta a floozy, but then I got to see her in action around a group of boys, and I wasn't so sure.

I began to have doubts about Gusta the day she led me down the path to sin, which at the time, I was sure would lead me straight into Hell. I admired her audacity, but I thought she went too far when she tempted Pete, Adam, and Henry with hints of carnal gratification, although I was impressed when she dashed their hopes and completely embarrassed them. I sure got an eyeful that day. Ruby wouldn't have gone that far, and Mother would have been horror-struck. I doubt that Gusta, even with all her charm and manipulation, would have gone unscathed if Mother discovered that she introduced me to the more tawdry side of life.

Every summer, Ruby and I tented overnight with our Campfire Girl friends. Our leader, Mrs. Johansson, set the date for the fourteenth of August at the Wisconsin River, and Dad agreed to relieve us of milking duties that night and the next morning. He said we deserved a reprieve after helping in the fields all week. When we asked Gusta to join us, she declined. "I don't have time for a day with giggly girls. I'm going out with the boys. I've got a lesson to teach. But if I get bored, I'll join you later."

Ruby thrust her nose in the air. "Well, la de da. You'd better not let Mom hear you talk like that."

"I know better than to say that in front of Aunt Mary."

"Coward."

"Would you say that in front of her?" Gusta said.

"No, but I'm going camping with those giggly girls."

"Oh, Ruby," I said, "she doesn't know the fun she's missing. If she did, she'd join us."

"Don't you worry about me finding fun," Gusta said. "But I was just joshin' you. I'm going into town to teach Sheri Derryberry the two-step."

When I entered the house, I heard Gusta tell Mom, "I promised Sheri I'd stop over. She's having trouble with the two-step, and I said I'd help."

But Mom remembered Gusta's late-night episode. "Your month's not up yet, so you're not going off on your own. You must earn that right again."

I could almost see Gusta's brain whirling, and before Mom returned to her dusting, Gusta said, "Can I go if I take Catherine along?"

That caught my attention. Gusta was wily. I suppose she thought Mother would believe she wouldn't do anything too outrageous if I was along to tell the tale.

"Can I go, Mom? I need the dance practice, too."

"You know Sheri can't find a beau," Gusta said. "She's kinda plain, but I thought this might help her."

I knew that Mother had a weak spot in her heart when it came to helping people—Gusta knew it, too.

"That's considerate of you, Gusta," Mother said. "But I expect both of you to be at the campfire before nightfall. You can take Fanny Too and Lyda. I'll pack sandwiches and some raw veggies."

"Can it be a cheese sandwich, Aunt Mary?"

While Mother buttered the bread and cut large slabs of Swiss cheese, Gusta whispered to me, "You might be sorry."

As Gusta walked toward the barn to saddle the horses, Ruby said to me, "I didn't think Mother would let her go, not yet anyhow. Gusta gets out of messes as easily as she gets into them. I get into messes easy enough, but I don't have the back-end figured out yet."

"You're just jealous," I said.

Ruby frowned. "Yeah, I guess so."

And we went to Sheri Derryberry's and practiced the dance. Afterward Gusta said that she was pleased with her day so far, and I agreed. Sheri had learned the dance quite smashingly, and I improved, too. And now we were headed toward the campsite, or so I thought. I wanted to get there early because we had the most fun before Mrs. Johansson arrived for the night. But Gusta turned away from the river and headed in the opposite direction. "Catherine," she said, "I've got an appointment to keep. Remember, you wanted to come along."

"Aren't we going to the campfire?" I said. "Ruby will be upset if we don't show up."

"We'll go there, but first, I've got a rendezvous at the quarry with three horny boys who think they can bamboozle this Texas girl. They've got a lesson to learn, and I'm the one who'll teach it." She grabbed my arm to slow me down. "And you'll be learning a few things, too, but don't you dare tell anyone. 'Cause if you do, we'll both be in the shithouse."

I blanched at the words. I knew that Gusta would swear, but she'd not been so brazen in front of me before.

She grabbed my arm. "Do you swear silence?"

I knew we were headed for trouble, but I'd had lots of experience with Ruby, so I said yes. But I was nervous about it.

"Now, you stay back and watch me maneuver. But turn your head if it gets too—well, you'll know. I don't want Aunt Mary to hear that I introduced you to sin."

Pete Simmons, Adam Baxter, and Henry Laurie were at the quarry when we arrived. I knew the boys, and I didn't much like them.

Pete looked at me. "What's she doing here?"

"Don't you worry about Catherine. She's my second. All combatants have a second. You know that. It's the rule of the realm. You have Adam and Henry."

"Huh?" Pete said. He didn't look convinced, but he did look confused.

"Did you bring the cards, boys?" Gusta said.

"Cards?" Pete said.

"You want to play cards?" Henry said.

Pete straightened his pants. "Gosh, no."

"Now, boys," Gusta said, "you didn't think I'd meet you here for immoral purposes, did you? I'm surprised you'd think that badly of a lil' ol' Texas girl." She tossed her hips. "Why, back home, Texan men would never misinterpret a girl's honorable intentions. Aren't you Wisconsin boys more gallant than that?"

The three boys blushed and dug their hands deeper into their pockets.

"Oh, no, we'd not think that," Henry said.

"We know you're a Southern lady," Pete said.

"That's okay, boys. I thought there might be some misunderstanding, so I brought my own deck." Gusta pulled a deck of cards from her saddle bag. "Boys, you know how to play strip poker, don't you?"

I was no longer sure I wanted to be there. But I didn't want to leave either. I'd never seen boys so eager around a girl. They assured her they knew exactly what she was talking about.

"We're going to play strip poker, Texas-style. I call it stripjack. I'll give you a fightin' chance to get what you came for. You want to see me naked, don't you? 'Fess up."

Oh, my god! Sharon was right about our cousin. She was a hussy.

Pete turned a deep shade of red. "Well, Miss Gusta … you … I—"

"That's okay, Pete, but you'll have to earn it."

"I knew you was a sportin' lady when I first laid eyes on you," Henry said as he reached for the deck.

Adam hung back.

I turned my head, but Gusta whispered in my direction, "Don't you worry, cousin. Just watch this Texas girl outsmart these country hicks."

I was fascinated, but I knew I shouldn't be here.

She returned her attention to the boys. "Bring the cards, and I'll show you how to play Texas stripjack."

"Texas stripjack? What's that?" Pete said.

"Do you know what blackjack is?" Gusta said.

"Well, yeah, kinda," Adam said. "Don't they call it twenty-one?"

"Sometimes, but I call it stripjack 'cause I plan on stripping you to your birthday suits."

I couldn't believe my ears.

"Better call it stripjane 'cause there're three of us," Adam said. "We own the odds."

"We'll see," Gusta said.

The boys gathered around.

"So you'll get some practice," Gusta said, "we'll play a few games for pennies before we do the big stakes." She looked Pete in the eye and smiled a wicked smile.

She is a hussy, I thought.

"We'll take turns dealing. The dealer must take a card on anything under seventeen and must refuse a card on seventeen or higher. Got that?"

The boys nodded.

"Anyone who beats the dealer gets double the pennies he bets," Gusta said. "If the dealer wins, you lose your money. When we get to the main event, we'll shed more than pennies. Understand?"

The boys nodded again, this time with smirks on their faces.

"One more rule. Before the main event, we'll empty our pockets. Nothing can be taken from a pocket. Okay?"

The boys stared with blank expressions.

"And another rule. So that no one panics and runs, Catherine will tend the discard pile." Gusta looked toward me. "Catherine, stuff all the discards into my saddle bag."

In unison, the boys retreated a step.

"What's the matter? Afraid you big, tough men will lose to a lil' ol' Texas cowgirl? And there's only one of me."

The three boys vigorously shook their heads. Pete said, "Okay, we'll empty our pockets, but you, too, Gusta."

"Of course, I wouldn't have it any other way. Pete, you deal. We'll play the first hand, cards up. To learn the game."

Pete dealt himself a five on top of a queen. He dealt Gusta a six and a king. "I don't think I can win with sixteen," she said. "So I'll take another card."

Pete dealt her a three, and she won with nineteen over Pete's bust. "See, you've gotta take chances to win," she said. "It takes luck, but you've gotta have guts. Do you have the backbone, boys?"

They continued to play for pennies. Gusta took cards when holding hands of twelve through seventeen, even when the dealer showed a four, five, or six. She lost a lot of pennies, but the boys didn't do much better. What they lost on the play, they won back on the deal, including some of Gusta's pennies.

It was clear they were outdoing Gusta. I was worried and decided it was time to go. I started toward my horse, but Gusta grabbed my arm. "Sit tight, Catherine. You watch; my luck's about to change."

"I think it's time we played stripjane," Pete said. "I'd like to see more of Gusta than we've seen so far."

"Lot's more," Henry said as he poked Pete in the ribs. "We're friendly guys, aren't we, Pete?"

"Sure are. We'll show you our stuff, Gusta," Henry said.

Adam snickered. "I think it's Gusta who'll be doing the showing. Right, Gusta?"

Gusta knew I was wavering. She grabbed my arm again and held on.

"We'll see, fellas, we'll see. High card deals—go ahead, Pete. But just one second before you start. Remember, empty your pockets. That's a house rule. Everything else you're wearing is fair game, though."

"You, too, Gusta. Fair is fair," Henry said.

"Sorry, boys, I don't have any pockets, but just to show you I'm a good sport, I'll empty my purse." She proceeded to empty a few pennies, bobby pins, matches, and a package of cigarettes on the ground. "That's the beginning of my disrobe pile, boys."

She motioned for me to take the discarded items to the saddle bag.

"See, she's a sportin' lady," Adam said. "Go head and deal, Pete. I'm wantin' to see skin."

"You're going to, Adam," Gusta said as she played with the top button on her blouse. Maybe more than you bargained for."

The boys continued to play a reckless game, but Gusta changed her strategy. She refused hits when the dealer held a four, five, or six, and she held on twelve through sixteen. She never took a hit if she held a total of seventeen unless one of them was an ace. But she lost hands, too.

"Okay, Gusta, take it off. What's it this time?" Pete said. "Another earring?"

I was so busy moving clothing that I had trouble keeping up with the game's flow.

"That's not fair," Henry said. "Earrings, broach, and belt. What else do you have before you take off clothes, Gusta? I thought you were a sportin' lady. We're almost naked, and you've not begun to disrobe. Where's the sport in that?"

"I guess it depends on whose clothes you're wearin', doesn't it, Henry?" Gusta laughed. "Or how many are in your disrobe pile. Luck of the cards, boys."

I began to feel better, but I averted my eyes as the boys continued to disrobe.

Gusta received a six and the dealer an ace. "Doesn't look good, boys," Gusta said as she started to unbutton her blouse.

"Gosh, Pete, I've not seen boobs before," Henry muttered as he turned away.

"You see them every morning and night," Pete said.

"Well, those don't count," Henry said. "They're only cows."

"How'd you know the difference?" Pete said.

"I've snatched Dad's *Police Gazettes*. And they have pictures."

The boys got so excited that they called for hits on their nineteen and twenty, and both went bust before the dealer showed his cards. When Gusta went bust, too, she slowly reattached her top button and slipped another ring unto her discard pile.

I could see that Gusta was way ahead of these boys.

"C'mon, Gusta!" Pete said. "How can we win if you only discard jewelry?"

"Boys, I never planned on you winning. I don't play this with everyone, just those I know I can beat. Those who need a little humbling. My deal."

Down to their long johns, the boys began to squirm and cower.

"Now that I'm dealing, you're on the short end of the stick, boys. I think you're gonna see some skin—each other's."

"Aw, Gusta."

"Not what you had in mind, is it?"

Henry jumped up and started toward Gusta's saddle bags. "Gusta, have a heart."

Gusta stepped between him and her horse. "Just like you would—eh, Henry?" When she stood her ground, Henry turned away. "Sit down, Henry. You'd better stick to your *Police Gazette*."

Gusta paused before dealing the cards in her hands. "Boys, I have no hankerin' to see more skin. Your long johns are grimy enough for my taste."

"Aw, Gusta. That's not ladylike," Pete said.

"I'm seldom called a lady. But no one ever called me dumb either. You better learn to play before you do this again. There's a method to this game that you haven't quite mastered. And it helps to have lots of clothes. Good thing we weren't playing in December. Goose bumps on your privates could be interesting. Maybe I wouldn't be so generous."

The three boys blushed crimson. "Can we put on our clothes?" Adam said.

"I'll make you a deal. If you'll help me awhile this evening, I'll let you off the hook."

"Anything," the boys said in unison as they scrambled for their clothes.

We arrived at the river just before dusk. Gusta tethered Fanny Too and Lyda half a mile away, saying she didn't want the campers to hear us. She told me to stay behind her. We crept toward the girls who sat around a campfire. I could see that the adults hadn't arrived yet. As prearranged, the boys dispersed in a semi-circle near the unaware campers and began a series of animal calls that first sounded like a marauding big cat, soon followed by the bleat of frightened sheep. Maybe the boys couldn't play cards, but they sure knew their animal calls. I'd never heard such caterwauling.

Ruby jumped up. "What's that?"

Three girls grabbed their gear and ran in the opposite direction of the sounds.

"Wait," Ruby shouted. "We don't have big cats in Wisconsin."

"Grandpa said we used to," another girl said. "He said he'd be surprised if they don't come back someday."

Three more vicious yowls, closer now, convinced the remaining girls that Grandpa knew best. Standing alone, Ruby looked toward her fleeing campmates. One more yowl sent her after them, and she passed them all before they reached the adjacent hayfield.

Gusta and the boys howled their delight. Adam, Henry, and Pete declared that Gusta was a sportin' lady after all, even if she did bamboozle them in a card game.

"Mom says all's well that ends well, so I'd say this was a good day," Adam said.

Henry turned toward Gusta. "Can't I have one little peek?" he said as he reached toward her blouse.

A hard right cross landed him on his rear end.

"You play the hand you're dealt, and that wasn't in your cards today, my fine Yankee friend," Gusta said as she turned toward Fanny Too. "I'm afraid you've got a few more years with your father's *Police Gazette*."

Three days later, Mother called Gusta to the kitchen. "Dad found a card deck in Fanny Too's saddlebag yesterday. You're the last one to ride her, so we supposed they're yours. We talked it over, and although we've never allowed cards in our home, we decided we'd rather have you playing here than out behind the barn."

"Gee, Aunt Mary, you'd do that for me?"

But Gusta never again played cards in Wisconsin. When Ruby asked if she'd teach her some games, Gusta refused, saying, "Crime's just no fun when it's legal." But that was only half the story. I was too embarrassed to tell anyone what happened at the quarry. But I was glad to have been there to see her outwit those nasty boys.

12

A BIT TOO MUCH THIS TIME

Author's Note

Mother wrote, "Alice and I took many trips when we had vacation time. She was still working in the Dodgeville hospital as supervising nurse. One time we went to Grand Island, North Platte, and Kearney, Nebraska, where my grandparents' Fitzsimons relatives lived. We took my Grandmother Fitzsimons and Uncle Ira, my father's brother, with us. While there, Grandma didn't feel very good, so Irving's wife, Alice, who was a Fitzsimons before marriage, offered her some good cherry juice that she had made from her cherry tree in the back. Because Grandma was a teetotaler, Alice didn't tell her that it was cherry wine. Grandma drank it and kept saying that it made her feel so good. We all had to laugh, because she was so against any liquor."

When I was visiting relatives in St. Louis, they told me their cherries had fermented on the tree, and the birds began to act tipsy, which became the source for Gusta's justification for the girls actions in my story.

I couldn't resist writing this into a story. And who better to have as a foil for Gusta and Ruby's deviltry than the self-righteous, judgmental Grandma O'Shaughnessy?

Now don't go thinking that Gusta reformed her ways. While Ruby's sins were venial, Gusta's edged dangerously close to being mortal. Not long after Gusta gave up cards, she took up a more insidious vice. I didn't know about it until the weekend that Grandma O'Shaughnessy

PUPPET ON A STRING

visited. I ate apples, plums, pears, and cherries in summer and fall, and I helped Mother can preserves throughout the year. I didn't believe Gusta when she said that people made liquor from these wonderful fruits.

When Mother told us that Grandma O'Shaughnessy was coming for the weekend, I forgot about fruits and liquor. Sharon's beau, Ed Meadows, would drive her here in his buggy. When Grandma O'Shaughnessy visited, you tended to forget everything else.

I was exiting the henhouse with a basket of eggs when Ruby rushed from the barn and grabbed my arm and announced Grandma O'Shaughnessy's visit.

"Mother said that Ed will pick her up on his way here," Ruby said. "You know what that means. She'll arrive with a headache. Long buggy rides always give her a headache."

"I'm glad Dad pulled a cot into Sharon's room and not ours." I grimaced. "She'll be crabby as blue blazes until tomorrow morning, but she likes Sharon."

"I sure hope Gusta doesn't smoke a cigarette in front of her. You know how Grandma hates smoking and spirits," Ruby said.

"Or a swear word," I said. "Oh boy, Mom and Dad would never hear the end of it if Gusta swears. Maybe Mom will send Gusta to visit her friend Sheri."

"Life would be easier for us all."

When we heard the buggy approach, Mom, Sharon, Ruby, and I ran from the house. At first, Gusta held back. Mother had given permission for her to smoke if she had to, but not inside the house. As I feared, Gusta exited the house with a cigarette in her hand and lit it just when Ed's buggy stopped at the front steps.

Grandma O'Shaughnessy looked toward Ed, and then back to Gusta. "Who's that? A new farmhand? Will should know better than to hire someone who smokes, and a girl at that." She clasped her hand to her head when she rose too fast before exiting the buggy. "My head's killing me."

Mother took Grandma's hand and helped her down.

"Oh, Mary, can I lie down for a while?" Grandma said. "This headache'll be my undoing. I just can't take these long rides anymore."

Sharon took Grandma O'Shaughnessy's arm and led her inside.

"I can't remember when she didn't get headaches," Ruby said to me. "I think we should visit Sheri, too. It'll be a long weekend."

"Who's that?" Gusta said.

"Grandma O'Shaughnessy," I said. "She visits twice a year. Mom's nice to her, but Dad stays in the barn most of the time. The coward."

"Looks to me as if her girdle's laced a bit tight," Gusta said, exhaling smoke.

"She's okay," I said. "She's just tired and has a headache. She always comes with a headache. She doesn't like long buggy rides."

"I bet that's not all she doesn't like. Could use some loosening up, I think."

The supper table was uncharacteristically quiet. Even Dad, who usually kept the conversation flowing, was mostly silent. Only Gusta, now introduced as a family member, seemed her jovial self.

She just doesn't know better, I thought.

"Mrs. O'Shaughnessy, you had a long ride today. About as far as we go to get liquored up in Texas," Gusta said, and then laughed.

I thought she was putting Grandma on.

"Course, our women ride horses every day, so they're used to it."

Grandma O'Shaughnessy reddened. "You mean they ride in a buggy every day, don't you, young lady?"

"No, they ride horseback," Gusta said. "Just like Ruby and Catherine, they love sitting on a good horse."

"But Ruby and Catherine are children."

Ruby grimaced.

"Wisconsin women ride in buggies," Grandmother O'Shaughnessy said. "It's more ladylike."

"I don't mean any offense, ma'am. Our old geezers ride in buggies, too—at least those who don't get around much anymore. The able ones would be embarrassed to admit they're too old for a horse. But that's our Texas way. Yankee women aren't as hardy, I guess."

Mother held up her hand. "That's enough, Gusta."

"I'm sorry, Aunt Mary, but that's the way it is in Texas. I don't know how we ever lost that war."

Grandma O'Shaughnessy muttered to herself before turning to Mother. "I'd like to turn in now. My headache's getting worse."

Sharon led Grandma O'Shaughnessy upstairs.

Her headache persisted the next morning. And when she didn't come down for dinner, Mother sent me upstairs to see if she might want food brought to her bed.

"Maybe I'm coming down with something," she said to me when I looked into her room before heading downstairs. "Will you tell Mary that I'll stay in bed? I'd hate to bring whatever I've got downstairs."

I raced downstairs to tell Mother. "I bet she'd change her mind if you sent Gusta to keep her company," I said.

A faint smile crossed Mother's lips. "It's probably best to keep those two apart." But I still liked the idea. "Go to the orchard and pick a pail of cherries," Mother said. "I think some fresh cherry juice would help her feel better."

I was only a few steps from the house when I met Gusta coming back from the barn with a pitcher of newly skimmed cream from the morning's milking. "Aunt Mary wanted this cream," she said. "She's going to make plum preserves with scald cream for supper. She thought that Grandma O'Shaughnessy would like that."

I told Gusta that Grandma was still feeling under the weather and that I was going to pick cherries so Mom could make a medicinal cherry juice tonic.

Gusta walked past, but then she paused and turned back to me with a furtive grin and a raised eyebrow. "I don't think plain old cherry juice will fix her. But I've got an idea. Tell Ruby to meet me in the henhouse. We need to talk."

I couldn't guess what Gusta had in mind, but I knew that it was probably nothing good. After I returned to the house, I dutifully told Ruby to meet Gusta in the henhouse. Fifteen minutes later, Ruby entered the house alone and said to Mother, "Gusta wants to apologize to Grandma O'Shaughnessy for her rudeness last night. We thought that Grandma'd be friendly if Gusta and I took her the cherry juice. Maybe that'd get Gusta on her good side."

I knew that something was up, but apparently Mother was so eager to see a truce between her niece and mother-in-law that she threw caution to the wind. "Why, that's a splendid idea," she said. "I'll have it ready in a few minutes. You and Gusta can take it upstairs."

I knew that was a bad idea.

I followed Ruby as she headed toward the back stairwell carrying the pitcher of tonic. Gusta met her at the door, and I watched from behind the door as they held a brief discussion before Gusta continued up the stairs with the elixir. Ruby went outside. That's strange, I thought. Where's Ruby going? But I followed Gusta to Sharon's room.

"Hello, Mrs. O'Shaughnessy," Gusta said after she knocked and entered the room. "Aunt Mary prepared this cherry tonic for you to drink. She said it's the best thing she knows for a headache."

"Really? I've heard that cherry juice has medicinal properties."

"I think that Aunt Mary got this recipe from Daddy before he died. We use it all the time in Texas. We call it the wonder juice. Everyone drinks it." Gusta poured a glass of the cherry elixir. "I'm truly sorry for being a snot last night. I hope this'll make up for my rudeness." She handed the full glass to Grandma O'Shaughnessy.

By now, Ruby had joined us in Sharon's room.

"I guess I shouldn't be too surprised," Grandma said. "You are from the Wild West." She took a sip. "This is good." She raised the glass and drank a long time. "I think I feel better already."

Ruby looked at Gusta, who grinned back.

This is strange, I thought.

"How much should I take?" Grandma O'Shaughnessy said.

"Some take a little, some take more," Gusta said. "It's just good ol' cherry tonic. Whatever you like is fine, I'm sure. Why, some Texans drink this stuff all day long even when they're not sick—to ward off the germs."

"Maybe just a bit more," Grandma said. Then she took another long swig from the glass. "I must tell Mary how it's helped."

Grandma O'Shaughnessy ripped back the sheet and dropped a foot to the floor; then, when she tried to step forward, she sank to her knee. "Ooh, I've been in bed too long. Here, give me a hand," she said as she staggered to her feet. "I feel a little dizzy." She reached out, but I didn't dare move, and Ruby stood frozen, as well.

"Maybe you'd better not go downstairs just now," Gusta said. "I think you need to lie down awhile longer. This tonic can make you feel good, but your body may not be ready yet."

"Nonsense. I've not felt so good since I was a girl." Grandma giggled. "Now, come here, Ruby. Give me your arm."

"Please, Grandma, lie down for a while," Ruby said. "Don't go downstairs. Not yet. Let the juice work its magic for a bit."

Grandma O'Shaughnessy poured the glass full and drank half of it.

She didn't even stop for a breath, I thought.

"Now, grils, I've not spent time with your smother. I must thank her for this juzz. I've never belt fetter. Ruby won't help. Come, take my harm, Cathwrin."

If I didn't understand before, I sure knew by now what Gusta and Ruby had done, and I was certain we'd soon be in trouble. But I didn't dare refuse Grandmother's command, so I took her arm and helped her toward the stairs.

Ruby glared in my direction.

Gusta grabbed the half-full glass. "I think I'll need this killer tonic before the night's over," she said.

Grandma entertained the dinner table. When she told stories about Dad's courting days, Mother turned red and I could see that she was embarrassed. But Gusta begged for more. Grandma giggled as she told a crude joke about the Kaiser and then led a stirring rendition of "Camptown Races." When she collapsed, her head on her empty plate, Mother said, "I think I liked her better sober." She turned to Ruby and Gusta. "You girls have some explaining to do."

"Strangest thing," Gusta said. "I saw starlings falling outa the cherry tree and acting crazy drunk this morning. Catherine, those cherries you picked must have fermented on the tree. It happens all the time in Texas."

I would have laughed, but Gusta was so serious that it seemed she believed her own whopper. Cherries fermenting on the tree? I never heard such a thing. Mother's scowl suggested that she agreed with me. Ruby and Gusta protested their innocence, and I was happy that Mother's interest at the moment was Grandma O'Shaughnessy. I wasn't up for more interrogation that night. I already felt a smidgen of guilt about my participation in the day's raucous events. By Mom's look as she headed up the stairs with Grandma in tow, I suspected that Gusta and Ruby would hear more about this. But I didn't want to be around to see their noses held tight to the grindstone, so I went to bed early.

The next morning, Grandma O'Shaughnessy staggered into the kitchen. "That juice worked wonders for a while. It sure tasted good. But when it wore off, all the devils of Hell moved into my head." She wrestled with a hardback chair. "I don't know whether to take more of the juice or go home to recover."

Later that day, Mother pushed Grandma into the buggy. "Ed, keep these horses moving as fast as they'll go."

I thought that Gusta had gone too far, getting Grandma drunk like that. And although I'd always admired Ruby for her daring, I thought Gusta was corrupting her as well. I was afraid their shenanigans were leading them into the fire, and I was feeling a bit singed, too. But I'll admit, Grandma's visit was lots more exciting this time. That Gusta sure knows how to rile things up.

13

GUSTA LEAVES WISCONSIN

Author's Note

Mother wrote, "Gusta finally went back to Texas, not finishing the school year. Life was too dull for her here, and she never felt completely at home in the North. She'd say, 'Northern people are as cold as their weather.'" Mother concluded, ". . .but we liked her despite our different backgrounds, and I know that she liked us, too."

I described Gusta's "last hurrah" in my book, *Bittersweet Harvest.*

Real-life Gusta went back to Texas but continued to correspond with the Fitzsimons family, and Mother spent two weeks visiting Gusta in Texas. Gusta married a Texas oil company chemist, Louis des Rets, an Argentine citizen.

Mother told me, "She, Gusta, always wrote to Mother (Mary in my stories) and seemed to have great respect and affection for her. Later, after the folks moved back to Mineral Point, Gusta and her husband came up and took Mother and Dad down to their home in San Antonio, Texas. They had only a small apartment in Pampa (where he worked in the oil fields), since their main home was San Antonio. They were real nice to my folks. They wanted my dad to go into the business of supplying cheese to the oil fields of Texas, but by then Dad thought he was getting too old to start up a new business."

Gusta and Louis eventually decided to return to Argentina. They wanted Alice (Ruby in my stories) to go with them, saying that nurses were in great demand down there. But she stayed in Wisconsin, believing her parents needed her assistance. Gusta and Louis drove north to visit Mother's family once more before their departure from New York Harbor. Then they were gone. My mother and her family never heard from Gusta again. Mother always wondered, "Whatever could have happened to Gusta?"

FRAYING
THE TIES

14

CATHERINE'S LIFE CHANGES FOREVER

Author's Note

I didn't know about Carl. She never said the name Carl—not until, at 93 years, Mother wrote her book, *From High on the Bluff*.

Mother was a first-year country school teacher at the time she met Carl and was teaching a school that was two miles from her parent's home in Ridgeway, Wisconsin. I call Ridgeway Logan Junction in my stories.

Mother wrote, "One Friday night after school, I was walking home to the folks when I met a tall, good-looking man who I knew was principal of schools in Ridgeway, although I had never been introduced to him. He came out on the road and spoke to me, and we got to talking. Soon he asked if he could see me sometime. So that's how I met Carl, and that's how it started. He took me to the prom, and we continued to date for almost a year."

I characterize Carl as the charming, witty, and electrifying Jonathon in my novel and tell about Catherine and Jonathon's first date, a date that captures her heart, but a date in which she discovers letters that lead to doubts as well. Although I've depicted Catherine and Jonathon's meeting much the same as Mother told about meeting Carl, I've fictionalized the dance scene and added the discovery of letters that sowed seeds of uncertainty that follow Catherine through the rest of her time with Jonathon.

This Friday began like all other days that winter. I trudged through snow drifts and barbed wire fences, heading toward my country school. I labored through the day teaching geography, reading, and math, but by day's end, I was thinking about the weekend I'd spend with Mom and Dad, but that didn't promise much excitement. I had clothes to wash and iron, and I knew Mother would need help in the house. Students dismissed, I followed the roadway to Logan Junction because that was easier walking. I was almost home when bells clanged, whistles blew, and fireworks filled the sky. My life changed forever.

Ruby was attending nursing school in Milwaukee when our parents lost the farm. About the time they moved to Logan Junction, she took a nursing job eight miles away in Dodgeville. Right out of school, she became head nurse in the local hospital, with a dozen older, more experienced nurses under her supervision. She was good, and everyone knew it. She'd graduated first in her class and represented Wisconsin at the American Health Congress, held in Atlantic City. She was offered jobs at Bellevue Hospital in New York City and other top East Coast hospitals, too. But Dad and Mother were in difficult financial straits, so Ruby came home to help out. Ruby was always there when we needed her.

A year after Ruby left for nurse training, I graduated from high school and joined her at the nursing school in Milwaukee. I wanted to be with her again. I should have known better. I only lasted a week. I couldn't stand those white walls, blood, syringes, and sick people all over.

I came back to Dodgeville to a teacher training program, graduated after a year, and took a country school position outside of Logan Junction, the village where Dad and Mother now resided. They lived in a house owned by my sister Sharon and her husband. I think the rent was low, and with Ruby's help, they got by. Ruby lived in the hospital where she worked, and her job kept her too busy to spend much time with us.

I wanted to help, too, but a country school teacher didn't make much money; I barely earned enough to pay my own expenses. But I came into town on weekends to get a good meal and help mother with the housework. And it was one of those trips home that turned my life topsy-turvy.

It was a cold winter, a winter in which snow piled halfway up the buildings. I'll never forget those long walks through the drifted snow. I trudged through knee-deep fluff that piled in drifts and swirled around my hips. For as far as I could see, snow covered the fields, but I knew beneath that snow there would be the brown stubble and black furrows left from the farmers' fall plowing. Even the fence wires were covered, and snow mounded over the posts. Like the pictures I'd seen of the Russian steppes, the land looked clean and white forever, as if God had absolved all earthly wrongs and laid a fresh canvas for sinners to paint a new beginning on. It was beautiful beyond my imagination. If only I didn't have to walk through it.

And I paid a price for each footstep that violated that pristine world. I stopped to catch my breath every hundred feet. Fences were the worst. From afar, it looked as if I could glide over the top, but close up, the barbed wire grabbed my clothes and pierced my mittens. If only the farmer had anticipated my journey and built a stile for my comfort.

Five days a week, I walked a mile from the solitary bedroom I rented at the Anderson's—my home Monday through Friday—to the little one-room schoolhouse. Each day, I started a fire in the stove—first paper, then kindling, and, finally, logs that I carried from the woodshed. The stove pipe snaked through the room, avoided a collision with the back wall by turning upward and escaping through the ceiling. Children learned to evade hot metal long before their first day in school. When the pipes turned red, I closed the damper to preserve fuel and avoid overheating. Once the dirty work was done and the temperature was rising, I shed my work clothes and changed into a dress that I kept in the schoolhouse until I took it home for washing at week's end.

With little time before the children arrived, I rushed the day's lessons from my burlap sack and laid them out on the desks—arithmetic, reading, language, and geography worksheets that I'd handwritten under a single light bulb the night before. It was my third year of teaching, and I had at least one student in each of the eight grades—a rare occurrence. I was thankful to have older students, as they helped teach the younger ones, but the extra worksheets were a chore. I seldom finished before midnight.

After the children left for home, I washed the desks and swept and mopped the floor before I trudged home for another night of worksheets. The work didn't bother me. I'd worked from sunup to sunset and beyond all my life. But no matter how hard I tried, I couldn't get ahead financially. I made so little money that my bank account crept upward slower than mercury on a frigid January morning. I loved books and wanted to be a librarian, so I'd completed the required year of teacher training to qualify for my first country school with the hope I could save enough money to return to college for a library science degree. But that dream looked more remote than ever.

On Friday, because I had no worksheets to worry about as I walked the two miles to my parents' house in Logan Junction, I walked slowly, concentrating on my finances. Half of my $150 a month went for room and board, and by the end of next summer, with no income, everything I saved would have melted away. After ten minutes of stewing over finances, I decided it was better to think about worksheets. With gloomy thoughts clouding my brain, I strolled toward home. My life was dull and routine. The work was so hard, but I had no choice; I needed an income, and Mom and Dad relied on Ruby and me now that they'd lost the farm.

Then everything changed. And it happened so unexpectedly. Even with fresh snow on the ground, the two-mile hike to Logan Junction wasn't as difficult as my trek to the schoolhouse each day because I could take the roads and walk the beaten path. I rounded the last curve and approached the village high school when I noticed a man standing by the main entrance. How I wished I had enough education to teach in town. There would be no cross-country hikes and no wood to carry, but better pay. However, if I had the money to complete that education, I'd have the money to earn a librarian's degree. I was so deep in thought that I didn't notice that the man was now standing by the roadside. I was startled when I heard, "Miss O'Shaughnessy."

I looked up to see a tall handsome man with dark wavy hair and eyes deep azure, like the blue in the pictures I'd seen of Yellowstone's Morning-glory pool.

"Oh."

I stopped so suddenly my feet almost slid from under me.

He gripped my shoulder to steady me.

I looked up into those morning glory eyes and gasped, so the words were barely audible, "How'd you know my name?"

The man flashed a broad, boyish smile that caused my heart to flip flop. "I've seen you walk past every Friday this winter. I asked my teachers your name."

I blushed. "You must be the school principal, Mr. ... "

"Hays. Jonathon Hays. And the choral, band, and physical education teacher, too."

I regained my composure and shoved my hand forward. "How do you do, Mr. Hays? I'm Catherine O'Shaughnessy, but I guess you know that."

Jonathon took a step forward. I backed up a step. "They say you teach at Spring Valley School," he said. "That's a long walk for those little Irish legs."

"And it's worth every step to get home for Mother's cooking."

"You live up on Main Street, don't you? Just down from the City Service station?"

I blushed redder this time. "You know an awful lot about me. I'm at a disadvantage. I know nothing of you."

"I'd like to change that. There's a high school ball a week from tomorrow. Will you allow me to escort you?"

"That's rather sudden. We just met."

"You needn't worry. We'll be chaperoned by forty or fifty students and a quarter of the town."

"I suppose … "

"Will you think about it then? Next Friday. Stop and let me know."

"But you won't have time to find someone else."

"My fate's in your hands."

Mr. Hays was an attractive man, and he seemed nice, too. But I thought he was awfully confident.

Just as he said, Jonathon arrived at my parents' house at five o'clock. The dance didn't begin until eight, but I'd agreed to dinner, and he wanted to get to the school early to help the band set up and to greet students and their parents. I couldn't imagine being a teacher and a principal in a big school. Of course, I taught academics, vocal music, and art; supervised recess; kept records; cleaned the building; and filed county reports. The one thing I didn't do was collect a principal's paycheck. I guess Professor Amundsen was right when she'd told us that country teaching isn't for everyone; the work is hard and the pay is low.

As we entered the school, Jonathon said, "Catherine, I'm going to clear the stage for the orchestra. The senior class was practicing its spring play when I left for your house."

"Can I help?" I said.

"Will you run to my office and get my class sheets? I'll send a thank-you note to the parents who're here."

"The kids'll die of fright when they see those envelopes."

"It'll keep them on their toes. The attendance sheets are in my top middle drawer. It's open. Just down the hall to the right."

I found the class sheets where Jonathon had said. As I checked to be certain I hadn't missed any, I noticed a stack of letters tied with a red ribbon. I looked more closely and could see that the top envelope was postmarked Cleveland and addressed to Jonathon in a woman's delicate handwriting.

I knew it shouldn't concern me, but I wondered just the same.

I ran back to the gym where I found Jonathon struggling with a bass drum and some snares. "Now I remember why I let students move the instruments," he said.

I grabbed two chairs. "Didn't you say you're a great athlete?"

"An athlete, yes." He flexed his muscles. "But I'm no weight lifter."

Boys, their hair slicked with mustache wax, and girls in their best— maybe only—Sunday dresses, began to slip into the gym. The boys clustered on one side of the room; the girls talked and giggled on the other. Even couples soon separated. The band played "I'll Be With You in Apple Blossom Time," but no one danced. During another song, "Sentimental Journey," a few parents drifted onto the floor, but there still were no student dancers.

"I'll have to do something about this," Jonathon said. He walked across the stage, motioned the band to stop, and then he faced his students. "Boys, girls, and parents, I would like for you to meet Miss Catherine O'Shaughnessy, who's here with me tonight."

I waved at both sides of the gymnasium and curtsied to the band. I knew a few people in town, but I didn't know most of these parents. Although I could feel my face redden, I liked it that Jonathon was thoughtful enough to introduce me.

"The next song will be, 'In the Good Old Summertime,' a waltz. Miss O'Shaughnessy and I will lead, and the students who follow will be excused from Monday morning's calisthenics.

A boy shouted, "We don't do calisthenics in physical education class anymore, not since Christmas!"

"That's right, Jake," Jonathon said. "But we'll start again Monday if you don't get your exercise on the dance floor tonight."

He held out his hand, and when I took it, he led me to the middle of the gymnasium. The band began, and Jonathon stepped forward with the strongest and smoothest lead I'd ever known. I'd danced with farm boys before, but it was never like this. I felt as if I were in the arms of a master puppeteer guiding my every move. We danced waltzes, two-steps, and polkas all night long. And the floor was full every set. There'd be no calisthenics on Monday.

The band played "Auld Lang Syne" at eleven o'clock, the designated ending time. I helped Jonathon gather trash and fold chairs, and at eleven-forty-five, he led me to my doorstep. What a wonderful man, what a glorious night!

"Jonathon, thank you for so lovely an evening. I'd like to do it again sometime."

Jonathon took my hand. "How about tomorrow?"

I'd stepped toward the door, but I turned back to face him. "Isn't that rushing—?"

"It may be proper to wait a week or so, but I have something that I must show you. I wanted to bring it tonight, but I couldn't."

Jonathon looked like a little boy, hang-dogged and cry-faced, pleading to go Christmas shopping with his parents. My heart melted at the sight.

"Please, just for an hour after church. I'm dying for you to see it. You won't be sorry."

I wondered what could be so important that I had to see it tomorrow. What a strange man. Wonderful, but strange. "It's broad daylight. I suppose ... "

Jonathon straightened and poked at my shoulder. "You silly girl. I'll pick you up after dinner. How about one-thirty?"

"I didn't—"

"I'll have you back in an hour," Jonathon shouted as he skipped to the car. "I promise."

A strange man, indeed.

The next day, I stepped into Jonathon's Ford Sedan Coupe at exactly one-thirty. "My dad sold Fords when we lived in Ashley Springs," Catherine said. "He was the first car dealer in town, but he left the business during the Depression." I frowned at the memory. "But he loved horses best. I think that's why he returned to farming, to get back to his horses. He knew more about horses than anyone in Iowa County. He refused to mechanize, even when everyone was buying tractors."

The smile on Jonathon's face was as broad as that on a jack-o-lantern after the knife had sliced too far east and west. "Not all horses are bays, not all cars are Fords," he said. Jonathon didn't say another word until five minutes later when we stopped by a small shed behind the Chevrolet agency, but the smile never left his face. He stepped off the running board, walked around the car, and gently lifted me down. Holding my hand, he led me to the sliding door.

"Close your eyes," Jonathon said.

"What?"

"Close your eyes," he said. "I'll tell you when to open them. Don't peek."

I placed my hands over my eyes, and then I heard the shed door slide back. "Okay, you can look now."

When I opened my eyes, I wasn't sure what I was seeing. It was an automobile but unlike any I'd seen before, even in pictures: long, low, sleek, and blue—but not a simple blue, but a deep blue like the waters of the deepest sea. The wheels were thin wire, tall and nickel-plated. A long narrow hood like the prow of a ship nestled between the wing-like fenders. The entire machine sparkled in the sunlight that flooded through the open door.

"What is it?"

Jonathon beamed like a kid showing off his first bicycle. "It's my Bug."

"A what?"

"It was made in France for the race circuit. There are only a few. It's a Bugatti. I call it my Bug."

I was spellbound. "It must be very expensive."

Jonathon nodded, and in a solemn tone said, "It is. I could never afford one, not on a principal's salary, not here in Logan Junction." He shook his head. "It belonged to Grandfather Hays. He'd made a fortune in land speculation after the crash. We didn't even know he had money until Grandma died. Then he went kind of crazy." Jonathon rolled his eyes. "He threw parties. He kept women. He bought a big house and this, too. Six years later, he had a stroke, and I got it."

"It's all yours?"

"Yep. I haven't even driven it yet. It's been stored because I can't drive on winter roads." Jonathon dusted the already spotless fender with his shirttail. "Grandpa'd come out of his grave if I were to dent it. I almost brought it out for the dance last night, but I thought better of it." He strutted around his Bug like a rooster circles his harem. "I had to show you today."

I ran my fingers over the huge headlights. "It must be terribly fast."

"Oh, it is. It's won races all over the world," Jonathon said. "Not this one, but others like it. Grandpa customized and rebuilt it to run on the highway; otherwise, it would never hold up to the rough roads we drive on. Even if I'm careful, it'll take lots of upkeep."

"Can I ride in it?"

"You'll be the first to sit beside me. Cross my heart."

I could hardly wait.

True to his word, after Jonathon had practiced enough to feel comfortable behind the wheel, one Saturday he drove to my house and honked his horn. He knew that Mom, Dad, and we girls would be home that day, and he couldn't wait to show off his treasure. Jonathon spent the afternoon answering questions and taking us for rides, but only one at a time—the seat wasn't wide enough to hold more than a driver and one passenger.

When Dad saw it, he stood with his mouth agape and scratched his head. "Praise be, those French sure do things pretty. It's a far cry from the Lizzies I sold, although it's got one thing in common with those old girls: it won't stop, either, when I holler whoa."

Jonathon cupped his fingers over the handbrake. "As long as you're sitting on that side, you can holler all you want. I'll do the stopping over here."

Jonathon, with his dark wavy hair and deep blue eyes, looked like every hero I'd ever read about or seen in the movies. He was my Wilfred of Ivanhoe, my Robin of Locksley, my Prince Charming. He was funny, gentle, and kind, just like my dad. Those first days together opened a new chapter in my life story, but they left me with doubts, too.

15

A TUMULTUOUS DAY AT THE PICNIC

Author's Note

Mother never said that Carl helped her with a school event, but he might have. It was a natural to include in my story as it related directly to a country school teacher's life—and it was a good way for me to expand Jonathon's character. It also gave me the opportunity to illustrate how harried a country school teacher must feel as she carries out her many responsibilities.

Ruby came home for a weekend and said that a new nurse from Minneapolis knew about Jonathon, said there was a scandal, a tragic accident—that Jonathon was tainted.

I thought about that stack of letters, but those were postmarked Cleveland. None of it made sense. I brushed it off at the time, told Ruby she shouldn't be telling rumors, but the news fueled my doubts.

I had little time to fret over it then. The school year was almost over, and my thoughts were on the year's last event—the spring picnic. And Jonathon said he'd help.

At the beginning of the year Mr. Thompson, the Board of Education's president, handed me a list of must-dos for the school that included janitorial work, a Christmas pageant, a graduation ceremony, and a spring picnic. The late-night preparations, teaching twenty-four students in eight different grades, and the daily house-cleaning chores had worn me to a frazzle, so I was glad for Jonathon's help with the year's last event. I decided to make the picnic a box lunch event, with the boxes to be auctioned off by Mr. Wagner, our local auctioneer. He agreed to help but said he'd have to leave early to prepare for his upcoming auction at the Marshal farm. And I had my students' parents to help me through the day. But I was exhausted trying to keep up with their urgent requests.

Maxine McMillan, carrying a tray full of boxes, caught me as soon as I stepped from the car. "Miss O'Shaughnessy, where should we put the box lunches?"

"Pull the picnic table from the shed and set them on that, Maxine."

When she sat the tray down and rushed toward the shed, I shouted toward Janet Reilly, who was about to enter the schoolhouse. "Would you get a tablecloth from the kitchen, Mrs. Reilly?"

I'd sent Jonathon to help with the picnic table and was about to follow Janet into the building when my second-grader, Ginny Mae Baxter, grabbed my arm. "Miss O'Shaughnessy, Tomcat and his friends are peeking in the boxes."

Geraldine Craft stepped from the building with a red-and-white-striped tablecloth in hand, and as she headed toward Maxine and Jonathon, now busy setting up and wiping down the picnic table, she asked, "Miss O'Shaughnessy, did you tell everyone to bring their own eating utensils?"

"I think I forgot to tell them, but there's silverware in the drawer next to the Frigidaire."

Ginny Mae tugged at my sleeve. "Oh, Miss O'Shaughnessy, I love your pretty pink dress. Pink's my favorite color."

"Well, thank you, Ginny Mae. Will you help Janet Reilly with the tablecloth?"

"Yes, Miss O'Shaughnessy."

"Looks like you need a janitor," Jonathon said.

"This is the life of a country school teacher. Will you tell Tomcat to come see me? He's the husky redhead in the green flannel shirt and red suspenders. He was in the schoolhouse last I saw."

Jonathon loped toward the schoolhouse door, and I headed to the backyard to help with the table. I hoped that it was big enough to hold all the box lunches. Now, if the auctioneer only remembered to come. I turned the corner and heard Tomcat shout at Ginny Mae, "You're a baby. You're little. You're a baby, Ginny Mae."

Ginny Mae threw a rock in Tomcat's direction. He dodged, eased backward, but watched her every move.

"You're mean, Tomcat! I'm not a baby."

"Tomcat, come here," I said.

But he bounded around the far side of the building.

"Miss O'Shaughnessy, he always makes fun of me. He's a nasty boy. If I could throw straight, he'd be sorry."

"Ginny Mae, you can't throw rocks. This is the last day you'll see him this summer, and he'll be in town school next fall, so you'll not see him all next year."

"Oh, Miss O'Shaughnessy, he makes me so mad. I'll get him yet."

"Miss O'Shaughnessy," Janet Reilly called. "Douglas is here with the ice cream. Where should we put it?"

"It's packed in dry ice, isn't it?"

Douglas nodded.

"Under the tarp in the back shed, out of the sun. But don't let anyone see you do it."

"Afraid the kids will eat it?" Douglas said.

"I'm more concerned they'll get burned on the dry ice."

A wood-paneled Ford station wagon pulled down the drive and stopped in front of the building. A man, a woman, and five girls exited and walked to the back. The man opened the tailgate and began handing stringed instruments to the girls.

"Mr. James!" I yelled. "Wait a minute. We've decided to hold the auction before the entertainment." I rushed to their car, took the violin from the littlest girl, and handed it to her father. "Mr. Wagner has to leave early, so we'll auction at eleven-thirty. It might be best to leave the instruments in the car until afterwards. There're lots of children running around, and I wouldn't want them damaged."

"Miss O'Shaughnessy! Help!"

I looked up just in time to see Tomcat chase Ginny Mae around the corner of the schoolhouse. He thrust a cardboard box toward her as he lumbered in her direction.

What could be in the—?

On the second go-round, Ginny Mae shouted, "He's got a rattlesnake!"

Ginny Mae increased the separation with each lap around the building.

Good thing for Ginnie Mae that Tomcat's slow, I thought.

The next time Ginny Mae came round, I stepped between her and the charging Tomcat who almost toppled when he skidded to a stop inches from my feet. Before I could grab the box, Tomcat regained his balance, turned, and ran, ignoring my demands for his booty. I turned to the frightened girl.

"There was a snake in that box, Miss O'Shaughnessy. I saw it. Tomcat said it was a rattlesnake."

"I doubt it, Ginny Mae. No one's ever seen a poisonous snake this far south of the bluffs."

"Maybe he went there and got it."

"Not Tomcat. He's not that ambitious. Go and play, but stay away from him."

"Miss O'Shaughnessy," said Mrs. Kincaid. "I can't keep the kids from under that picnic table. They're going to pull the tablecloth down and all the lunches with it."

"I'll look to it."

I looked for Jonathon, but didn't see him, so I headed for the picnic table to check the valuables that would help pay for new music books next fall. When I approached the lunch boxes, I thought that I saw a hand reach up from under the tablecloth, so I hurried toward the other end.

"Miss O'Shaughnessy," said Mrs. Jones, "you must do something about those men out back. They're spitting tobacco on the grass, right where the children are playing ball. Such a dirty habit."

"I'll be right there, Mrs. Jones."

When I turned back toward the table, Tomcat ran from the opposite side, and he had a lunchbox in his hand. "Tomcat, I've had enough from you today. Come here."

Once again, he ignored me.

"Miss O'Shaughnessy," Mrs. Jones called, "those men."

"Yes, Mrs. Jones."

I was beginning to feel frazzled as I raced toward the backyard. I hadn't planned on being the picnic's policeman as well as its janitor. "Fellas, if you must chew snuff, please do it off school grounds."

Where could Jonathon be? I walked into the schoolhouse, and there he was, in the back, spreading thick, white frosting on a marble cake.

"These ladies commandeered me," he said when he looked up and saw me. "They needed help to get these cakes ready for the auction. They warned that I'd better make them look pretty, because the pretty ones bring the highest bids." He carefully pushed a glob of silky sugar across the top of the cake. "Just like a pretty girl, I suppose."

The ladies watched and tittered while Jonathon performed his magic. "Mr. Hays, I'd think you were a baker," Sarah Smith gushed. "Why, I do believe we'll get the best prices ever for these beautiful cakes."

The other ladies nodded in agreement.

It's not just the beautiful cakes that turned these women to blabbering fools, I thought. But the cakes did look nice—another plus on the ledger for this charming man.

I heard a voice shout, "Miss O'Shaughnessy, come quick! Something's wrong at the outhouse. You'd think it's coming off its foundation, such banging and screaming you've never heard."

I ran from the schoolhouse and toward the back, near the evergreen grove where the privy nestled behind the trees. From a distance, I could hear thuds and screams, and saw a two-by-four pushing through the large vent screen. When I circled the little building, I saw immediately what was wrong. Someone had wedged a large branch between the door and ground, and I had no doubt about who was trapped inside. And I was certain that I knew who did the wicked deed. "Ginny Mae, is that you in there?"

"Yes, Miss O'Shaughnessy."

Just a second, Ginny Mae. I'll get this open."

Ginny Mae walked out, the two-by-four in her hand.

"That nasty Tomcat." She threw the board down. "He said I couldn't get out all day, that I'd miss the party."

"Ginny Mae, where'd you get that board? You've almost pushed the whole vent screen out."

"It was real loose, so I tore it off the wall. I was going to stand on the seat and climb through the hole when I made it big enough. I'm sorry, Miss O'Shaughnessy."

"Well, I suppose you had to get out somehow. It's about time for the auction. "Come with me, Ginny Mae."

Mr. Wagner stood behind a picnic table piled with attractively decorated boxes, plates full of cookies, and the cakes that Jonathon had helped adorn. He looked across the table toward a lawn full of young girls decked out in pretty spring dresses and eager young men, money in hand, ready to bid for the box they were certain belonged to the lady of their choice.

"Gentlemen, what do you bid for this box with the lovely pink ribbon?" Mr. Wagner called. "Why, I'd bid on it myself if I didn't have to leave before the eating starts. Do I hear one dollar? Fifty cents, then. It's a steal at fifty cents. Remember, the money you pay will reduce your property tax next year. Fifty cents, I hear." He pointed into the crowd. "Over there. Seventy-five, now. Do I hear a dollar? One dollar, I've got. Dollar-fifty over there." He pointed in the opposite direction. "One seventy-five, in the back," Wagner chanted.

Jonathon's five-dollar offer for my lunchbox brought the bidding to a halt. But I wasn't surprised, even though the prior bid was only three dollars. It was Jonathon's style to be flamboyant. And I loved that as much as his gentleness.

The auction over, Mr. Wagner hustled toward his car while the winning bidders, leading their ladies by the hand, tried to find unoccupied places on the school grounds.

"Come on, Jonathon, let's eat under the trees. I need to get away from the kids for a while. They'll be so busy eating that they'll leave me in peace—maybe."

Jonathon took my hand as we walked toward the back. "Be discrete, Jonathon. Remember, I'm the teacher, and I must be respectable."

"Don't be a prude, Cathy." He dropped my hand. "If I must, I'll behave, but only until we're hidden behind the trees. I can't wait to see what you've packed this time." He shook the box. "Is there corn relish in here?"

"Jonathon, you'll be proper—even behind the trees. These kids are everywhere. I'll still need an income next year."

I tried to spread a blanket behind the fir with the lowest hanging branches, but struggled when a gust of wind whipped it through the air. Jonathon grabbed the flapping blanket, and together we lowered it to the ground. "Cathy, what's that odor? We must be too close to the privy. Let's move away."

"Oh, Jonathon, I don't have much time."

He picked the lunch box off the ground but quickly set it back down. "Jonathon, what's wrong?"

I grabbed the box from his hand, and when I raised it to my nose and sniffed, my face started to burn. "Jonathon ... I don't know what ... " I opened the cardboard cover. "Eek! Who'd have done this?"

I turned the box over and half a dozen horse biscuits tumbled out. "This isn't my lunchbox."

Jonathon grabbed the box from my hands and tossed it down.

I burst into tears. "I made ham sandwiches with your favorite wine sauce. Watermelon pickles, too. I'm so embarrassed." I took a stick and pushed the biscuits into the box. "We can't leave them here."

Jonathon took the box from my hand and set it aside. "Who could have done this to you?"

"It's that awful Tomcat Runkin," I said. "I saw him under the picnic table. And I can't do a thing. He's already got his report card."

"He'll be in my school this fall," Jonathon said.

A screech came from the direction of the outhouse. Then a boy yelled, "Help! I bin bit!"

We rushed toward the screams and saw a half-naked Tomcat, his pants around his knees, stumble out the privy door and waddle through the weeds until his body outpaced his feet and he fell face-first into a thistle plant. He looked up as we approached. Spines punctuated his face and blood trickled from his nose.

Tomcat pointed toward the privy. "There's a snake in there. It dropped through the vent, right on my leg."

I held out the lunchbox, the one full of horse doo-doo. "Do you know anything about this, Tomcat?"

Tomcat struggled with his pants as he rose to one knee. "Not me, I don't know nothin', Teach."

"You've had quite a day," I said. "I should—"

"You can't do nothin'. I'll be in town school next year. You can't touch me."

"Oh, Tomcat. I don't think you've met my friend." I took Jonathon's hand and pulled him forward. "This is Mr. Hays. He's the town school principal."

Tomcat's lower jaw came unhinged.

"Hello, Thomas," Jonathon said. "Nice to meet you. I've got a feeling we'll see lots of each other come fall."

Tomcat stared blankly at Jonathon.

Just then Ginny Mae walked around the privy, an empty cardboard box in her hand. When she saw Tomcat cowering on the ground, she stopped, glared in his direction, and slowly wagged her finger as she said, "Poor, Tom. He's just a pussycat now."

The day left me exhausted, but I was grateful for Jonathon's help. How could I have any doubts about this sweet man?

16

NEAR DEATH AT THE BLUFF

Author's Note

Because Mother's father had lost the farm by the time Mother met Carl, it seemed reasonable that Mother would want to take him back, to show him the places she loved.

So I wrote the following story about Catherine and Jonathon. The day begins with Catherine and her father enjoying their time together; with Will commiserating with Catherine as she worries about Ruby's negative attitude toward Jonathon.

The day ends in near-tragedy when Jonathon risks his life to save Catherine's. Catherine's fondness for this brave man reaches a fever pitch—still, doubts linger.

I'd worked with Dad on the farm for most of my young life, but I never enjoyed time with him so much as those days in Logan Junction. We dug weeds and planted flowers. We talked about pruning roses and courting Jonathon. We laughed together, and sometimes we cried together, too.

I wanted a funny, kind man like my dad, and I thought I'd found him in Jonathon. I pushed doubts to the back of my mind and enjoyed our times together. I was glad that Ruby was so busy that she didn't have time to get home. But doubts wouldn't be vanquished so easily. Now and then, they leaked to the surface and trickled from my tongue.

I was home for the weekend, and it looked like a perfect day. The night's clouds had disappeared, and the morning sun lighted my room.

By seven o'clock, the dew had burned off the grass. The leaves on the shagbark hickory outside my window were as still as the hydrangea on my dresser. I knew there would be no kite flying today, and so I wondered what the day would bring.

I'd spent every weekend with Jonathon, and he'd agreed to pick me up at ten o'clock that morning. It would be my first trip to the farm since my parents had left more than a year before. I'd been afraid to face the old homestead, but I knew, with Jonathon, it would be a welcome reunion. It seemed like a perfect day for a picnic overlooking the river, and another beautiful day together.

But I wasn't sure. It was all moving too fast.

I packed a basket with ham and cheddar sandwiches smothered with fresh lettuce that I'd plucked from the garden that morning. My secret ingredient was a wine sauce mother had made—a topping that put the oink back into a slice of dry ham. The basket bulged with canned goods that had survived the winter's plunder: watermelon pickles, corn relish, plum preserves, and peaches. The night before, I'd picked asparagus spears, radishes, and winter onions—the garden's first yield that spring. I couldn't forget the salt. Jonathon liked salt on his fresh produce.

There were footsteps on the stairs, and I knew it must be Dad. He hadn't changed his lifelong habit of rising early, even when no cows demanded his attention. Life was so hard. Dad had worked all the time, but he'd never complained. People came to him for advice and asked him to head the co-op. That was his downfall—too many people had relied on him, and he felt that he'd failed them.

"Good morning, my dear daughter. Getting ready for your young man, now are you? I can see the excitement in your face."

"Oh, Daddy, he's just so … But I think he's getting serious, and I'm not ready for that—not yet, anyway. Ruby says he's too old, too sophisticated for me."

I didn't mention the rumors.

"Ruby wouldn't ask your permission, now would she? Only you know your heart, my dear Catherine."

"But that's the trouble, Daddy, I don't know. I think I love Jonathon, but he wants a big city job, and I'm not sure I'd like that. I've never lived in a cement world, and I'm not sure that I could. I love the outdoors and my horses. But I guess that's gone for good."

Dad's face fell, and I immediately wished I could take my words back. "I'm sorry, my dear," he said. "I made a terrible mess, now didn't I?"

"Oh, Dad, it's not your fault. I couldn't have lived at home forever."

"Well, if this is the one you want, you better grab him. You know what Aunt Net said about her nephew Joe, don't you?"

"No, Daddy."

"She said, 'He jumped over many a pretty flower and landed on a pissablossom.' So, take Aunt Net's advice and hang on to your Prince Charming."

And today he'd be my Prince Charming. But for how long?

Jonathon arrived at ten o'clock, just as I'd expected. After the fifteen-minute drive to Dodgeville, we turned north toward the Wisconsin River. Having been away for more than a year, I'd forgotten how beautiful the drive was in springtime. "Oh, Jonathon, look! The plum trees along Otter Creek are in full bloom. They only last a week or so, and they're peak color today."

"The gods painted them just for us, Cathy, to guide us to your Garden of Eden."

It was my Garden of Eden. I'd picked berries on the bluff and looked down on the farm and across the fields to the river. I'd watch Mom weed the garden and Dad cultivate corn. When I was up there, I felt like a queen on her throne.

"You know," I said, "Ruby and I would ride bareback through the fields, inhale the clover, fish the river, and sleep under the stars. I was unfettered and free. I never wanted it to end."

"Show me the places you loved."

"Oh, Jonathon, I will."

We descended toward the river, Jonathon threading his Bug through the narrow valleys. "I remember coming through here the first time. Mom, Dad, Sharon, Ruby, and I rode in one sleigh, and all our belongings were packed in four others."

"You took sleighs? All the way from Ashley Springs?"

"It took all day, but we were bundled in clothing and blankets and covered with straw to protect against the cold. Dad had heated soap stones the previous night and placed them at our feet."

"It sounds like something on a Currier and Ives print. Didn't you have a car?"

"Dad didn't want one. He was a horse man to the very end."

Jonathon shook his head. "I can't imagine horses pulling loads up these ridges. They're as steep as mountain roads."

I supposed the hills were so familiar that I hardly noticed anymore, but I remembered the tales. "Grandpa once pulled a two-story house half a mile up a hill as steep as these. I don't know how many horses he used; must have been a lot, though."

"I'm glad we have the Bug today. We no sooner drove into a valley, but another hill looms ahead. It's like the Coney Island roller coaster."

"Have you been to Coney Island?"

"Twice. The last time was a few years ago."

"I'll go to visit someday. To Coney Island, New Orleans, Pike's Peak, California—everywhere."

"Cathy, I want to take you. You won't believe New York City. It makes Madison look like Logan Junction. Thousands of automobiles, astonishing bridges, and buildings so high you can't see their tops."

I snuggled closer and took Jonathon's arm, but I didn't want to think about a cement world.

The Bugatti's tires skidded as Jonathon hit the brakes on a tight turn. "Whoa, I better keep my mind on the road, or we'll be steaming trout on the radiator. Is this the stream we crossed a mile back?"

"It comes off the ridge by Dodgeville and meanders between the hills and through the valleys all the way to the river. We're almost there."

We drove around a sweeping bend, and there it was. "See the willow trees. They're all along the river here."

I was almost home. Another fifteen minutes along the south bank, and I would be. I could smell the river, the willow shoots, plum blossoms, dead fish, and cow manure—a casserole of country perfume shouting, "You're home!" I stood and leaned over the windshield. "Hurry, Jonathon, hurry."

"Sit down, Cathy, and hold on."

Now on a straight stretch, Jonathon punched the accelerator, and cool air gusted over the windshield. I pulled off my scarf and let the wind comb through my hair, and I imagined racing Lyda along the river once again.

Jonathon slowed and pointed ahead. "Is that the bluff you picked berries on?"

"Oh, yes. Let's eat our picnic on top. It's a marvelous view. We can see the farm, the river, and all the places I've told you about."

"Where's the road?"

"There's no road."

"We walk?"

"What's the matter? Too high for a city boy?"

"Where do I park? I'll show you what a city boy can do."

"See the lane ahead? To the left, by that big oak? There." I pointed. "It winds through the thicket all the way to the top. You can park in that meadow at the bottom."

As soon as Jonathon slowed the car and pulled onto the grass, I grabbed the picnic basket and jumped out running, not slowing until he hollered, "No fair, Cathy! Give this city boy a fighting chance."

"A fighting chance you want, is it? Where's that great athlete you told me about? Cannae even beat a wee girl?"

I ran up the hill as fast as the basket allowed. I heard the car door slam, and in a moment, Jonathon's footsteps pounded the trail close behind.

"You're not so quick but what I can't catch you, my little vixen." He reached out and grabbed my arm, spun me around to face him.

"You had an unfair advantage. I'm carrying the basket. And besides, I wasn't really trying." I thrust the basket into his arms and raced up the lane once more.

Jonathon stood there and shouted, "I give up. You win. What's in this basket, anyhow? It's as heavy as a boat's anchor."

I stopped and faced him. "I said you had an advantage. You'll just have to wait until we get to the top, then you'll see what I packed. You'll like it."

Jonathon took my arm when he got alongside. "Cathy ... "

Something in his voice made me stop.

"These last three months have been the best of my life," he said. "You can't know how I treasure our weekends together, how I love being with you." He bent and kissed my cheek.

I blushed, but I must say I wasn't entirely surprised. "I'm the Irish woman. I'm the one who's supposed to be full of blarney, not you, a proper English gentleman."

"Don't make light of me, Cathy. I meant every word."

"I'm sorry, Jonathon. I've enjoyed them, too. I'm just … not sure of myself. I don't think I want to be serious yet. I don't know."

We walked arm-in-arm for ten minutes without saying a word. I knew that Jonathon felt rejected, and I didn't want that. But I didn't know what I wanted. I grasped his arm tighter as we approached the top, and when he looked down at me, his large blue eyes tugged at my heart. I didn't want a day that had begun with such promise to be dampened by my doubts, and I hated the silence, so I took Jonathon's hand. "Let's go to my lookout rock. We can see all the way to the river."

Jonathon came along, but he said nothing until we reached the top and saw the view below. "Cathy, it's spectacular. Did you come here often?"

As I took in the view, the same feeling I had as a kid washed over me: like a queen overlooking her kingdom. "See the farm down there, across the tracks? That was ours."

"With the road on this side?"

"Yes. You can almost see to the river. Isn't it magnificent? I used to ride down the lane to fetch the cows. See the lane? The poplars border it all the way to the water."

"That's where you rode Fanny Too?"

"And Lyda and Mabel. I miss it, Jonathon. I miss it so. It'll never be the same." I can't even help Mom and Dad like I should. How can I ever have property again?"

"Don't be discouraged, Cathy. It'll get better."

I didn't want to think about it. "Jonathon, let's eat our lunch here on my lookout rock."

Jonathon jumped down and ran toward where he'd left the basket. "I'll get it. I'll be back before you count to one hundred."

I reached eighty-eight.

"I'll spread the blanket while you unpack the basket, okay?"

A smile crossed Jonathon's face as he unloaded the goodies. "Cathy, I haven't had watermelon pickles since the Hays' family reunion, which must have been in high school. Mother never made them, but I sure liked them. Do you mind if I have an appetizer?" Without waiting for an answer, he twisted the lid off the jar and stuffed a pickle into his mouth.

"Ruby and I bottled them last fall. I'll make more when the watermelons ripen this summer, if you'd like."

He took a second crisp, sweet watermelon rind and savored it while the smile on his face broadened with each bite.

After a third, he said, "These are even better than I remembered. Promise me you'll make more, and you'll have my heart forever."

Just like a man. Isn't the quickest way to his heart through his stomach? But still, it gave me a strange thrill to hear him pledging himself to me, even if it were a joke.

"If you think the pickles are good," I said, "just wait until you try the wine sauce. After that, it's Mom you'll be wooing."

By now, I'd spread the cloth and set out the food. As we ate, Jonathon raved over each item. "I've always loved corn relish. This is delicious. The asparagus is perfect, as tender as baby green beans. I always seem to pick them after they're woody as a corn stalk."

"I bet you picked them by the roadside where you can't see them until they're too far along. We grow ours in the garden and pick every day." I opened the jar of wine sauce. "It's amazing how they'll shoot up overnight when the temperature and moisture are just right. But if you don't pick them fast, you'll be eating corn stalks."

"I never had a garden."

He spread some wine sauce on his ham and took a bite. "Oh, Cathy, I've never tasted ham so good! This sauce is ambrosia."

"It's Mom's secret recipe. She's never told anyone how to make it."

"You don't know how to make it?"

"No, I don't."

"Clearly, I'm courting the wrong O'Shaughnessy. This has been a rash infatuation. Do you think your mother would run off with a younger man?"

"Not one so silly. You're so full of blarney that I'd think you were an O'Shaughnessy."

"I'm no Mick, just an old English salt. The great-grandfather of my great-grandfather fought with Lord Nelson at Trafalgar. He was shipwrecked and died thirsty on an arid island."

"I hope he wasn't one of those Englishman who sailed across the Irish Sea."

"If by chance he did, I beg your forgiveness. In penance, I'll fulfill your every wish."

"You are a Mick. Okay, get me a drink of water."

Jonathon dug through the basket. "After all the salt I used on my veggies, I'm thirsty, too." He searched through the empty jars. "Did you bring water?"

"Isn't there a canteen in there?"

"Nothing. No water, no grog, not a drop to drink. You've sentenced us to a horrible death on your island in the sky. To die from thirst must be the fate of the Hays family. Now, it's you who must do penance. My wish is—"

"Mick. Mick. Mick. You sound like an Irishman. You could out-blarney Will O'Shaughnessy, and I grew up thinking he was the worst of all."

"Is there a spring nearby?"

"If we go down the backside of this bluff and walk about half a mile through Mr. Temby's cow pasture, an artesian well pours out the sweetest, coldest water you've ever tasted. But that means another mile's walk back to the car."

"Sweet, cold water? Only a mile and a half walk? So small a price for so great a treasure. What are we waiting for?"

We walked down the hill at a brisk pace until we reached a five-strand barbed-wire fence at the bottom. "This is Mr. Temby's cow pasture," I said.

"You're sure it's just cows, no bull?"

"He doesn't usually let his bull out of the barn. But it is spring."

Jonathon stepped back from the fence. "What do you mean, it's spring?"

I warmed. "Well, you know, spring. In spring, the birds and the bees …"

"So?"

"You know, the birds and the bees. In spring, thoughts turn to … love. Bulls, too, I'd imagine."

"What about Mr. Temby's thoughts?"

By the look on his face, I could see that Jonathon was thoroughly enjoying my discomfort. I slapped his arm. "Jonathon. I don't care about Mr. Temby."

Jonathon stopped smiling. "I may be a city boy, but I know that the bull can think whatever he wants; he's no danger to us while he's in the barn. It's whether Mr. Temby has decided to let him out that makes me nervous."

I understood his logic and looked across the pasture to the far side where the cows had found shade under the trees. I squinted to see if there was activity or any disruptive presence. Most were lying down, probably chewing their cuds after a morning of grazing. I reached for Jonathon's hand. "I don't see a bull, just contented cows. I think we can go."

"Okay, but keep a sharp eye."

He placed his left foot on the bottom strand of barbed wire and lifted the second, making a space which I scooted through. I did the same for him. At first, we walked warily, watching the herd as we moved across the field, but no animal even looked in our direction, so we soon lost interest. Besides, we were moving diagonally across the pasture, slowly distancing ourselves from the cattle.

We were about a hundred yards into the field when we saw him, a large animal lying behind a huge oak tree in the center of the enclosure. He had been hidden from view from the vantage point of where we'd crossed the fence. We froze, but it was too late.

The bull stood and faced us, his head close to the ground. He snorted softly and pawed the ground, scattering the grass. He raised his head and bellowed in our direction, a long deep call that sent chills up my spine. Then he slowly moved towards us. He was sizing us up.

"Don't move," Jonathon said. "Maybe he won't charge if he doesn't feel threatened."

I stood as still as my trembling legs would allow. I was probably more frightened than Jonathon. I knew what a bull could do. Years before, one had knocked Dad down and trampled and slashed him. Dad still had a slight limp.

The bull's head weaved side to side and his glistening nostrils flared open and closed as he sampled the air. Then he bellowed and loped toward us. The ground seemed to shake.

Jonathon pushed me back toward the fence. "Run, Cathy. Run to the fence. I'll distract him."

He grabbed the blanket from off the basket, waved it at the bull, and ran in the opposite direction.

At first I froze, my legs like Jell-O. I was frightened, mostly for Jonathon as he waved the blanket and raced across the pasture, whooping and shouting. I could see his objective: a wooden gate at the far side of the enclosure.

Jonathon raced ahead, but the bull gained with each thundering step. I knew I couldn't help from inside the pasture, so I grabbed the basket and retraced our steps, all the while praying, *Dear Lord, let Jonathon make the gate.* After I was through the fence, I'd work my way around toward Jonathon.

I still don't know how I got through that barbed wire without any help and not a scratch, but when I found myself on the other side, I looked back and almost fainted. The bull was no more than twenty paces behind, and Jonathon was a hundred feet from the gate. He wouldn't make it.

Then Jonathon did the unexpected. He darted left and parallel to the gate. Just as the bull was upon him, without breaking stride, he bent and picked a two-by-four off the ground, pivoted, and, with a mighty swing, clubbed the bull on the nose.

The bull dropped to his knees and slid past Jonathon, raising dust; but as fast as he went down, he jumped back up, whipped his head side to side, and bellowed loudly. But before he could resume the chase, Jonathon had vaulted the gate and landed face down on the other side.

I ran along the fence to where Jonathon lay on the ground. "Jonathon!" I said, panting heavily. "Jonathon! Are you okay?"

I took him in my arms.

He looked up, and his smile tugged at my heartstrings. "I'm okay, just winded. But if you'd like, I'll lie here awhile longer. I thought I was a goner until I saw that two-by-four on the ground. Thank God Farmer Temby didn't clean up his litter after building that gate."

"Thank God you're okay. I was scared."

"Don't tremble, my love. It's over."

And it was. The bull, satisfied that he'd protected his territory, ambled back toward the big oak tree.

I helped Jonathon sit up. "You're a hero, Jonathon. You saved my life. I'll never doubt your athletic ability again."

"You'll not see me run like that on a ball diamond, not unless the Barneveld Bulls' mascot sets after me." He gazed over my shoulder for the longest time, toward the horizon where cirrus clouds slow-waltzed across the distant sky. "I was a pretty good ballplayer once," he said. "Hitting that bull's nose was like hitting a grooved fastball, but I've never hit a home run that felt so good."

I heaved a prolonged sigh. "It didn't look easy to me, and I don't think it was. I doubt you ever lie in a heap after a home run."

Jonathon smiled. "Let's go get that sweet, cold water." He reached up and lightly kissed my lips.

This time, I didn't have a smart-aleck response. I was too busy kissing back. But I had a premonition that our destiny might not involve slow waltzes and adventures.

17

CARNIVAL ADVENTURES

Author's Note

Mother wrote and told about the many times she and her sisters attended events and enjoyed life together. One of her favorite accounts told about the harrowing experience she and Alice had when they went up in an open-cockpit airplane. "She wrote, "One day when I was working in Madison, Alice, Berniece and Amanza, and Anne and Earl and I went to the Dane County Fair. Alice and I decided to take a ride in an open cockpit plane. The pilot asked us if we wanted some thrills. We said that we'd wait until we got up there and let him know if we did. After we were up awhile, we thought that it was pretty nice so far, so Alice called up to him and said, 'We'll take those thrills now, mister.' And thrills we got. We went up and down, sideways, in loops and in circles. We couldn't get our breath. This was an open cockpit plane, and our head and shoulders were out in the 'wide blue yonder.'" She tells how she outmaneuvered her sister Alice to survive this harrowing experience.

That was an incident I felt compelled to incorporate into my Catherine and Ruby chronicle, an incident that culminates a day of frivolity and fun.

This story provides the opportunity for me to further develop the complex personality of Ruby and her interactions with Catherine, Sharon, and Sharon's husband, Ed. Serious, earnest Ed is a prime target for Ruby's harassment.

And—the story told about Catherine's father, his house, and Father McCrery really happened as told.

Jonathon told me that he wanted to get back to a large city, and I wondered what that would mean for our relationship. Would he still want me? Would he ask me to go? Could I live in a large city? Would I go?

He told me he was going to Chicago, but he said not to worry—that this was only an exploratory trip. He left Friday morning.

I was on my way home from school, but I hadn't yet reached Logan Junction High School. For the first Friday in five months, Jonathon wouldn't be there when I walked by. For the first weekend since the winter snow ball, I wouldn't be with him. As I rounded the curve south of town, I imagined Jonathon waiting for me to walk past. Today the school yard was as empty as my heart.

But I had other things on my mind, too. I hoped Dad would be home. Mom said he spends far too much time at Kelly's Bar.

Ed and Sharon had invited me to go with them to a carnival in Ashley Springs the next day. Ruby was coming home from the Dodgeville hospital for the first time in a month. I knew she'd be there when I got home, and we'd have a busy day the following day at the carnival, but that would be an unsatisfactory substitute for a weekend with Jonathon. Especially since Ruby wasn't the same carefree sister she'd always been. She didn't care much for Jonathon, and she let me know it.

"Ah ha!" Ruby called as I entered the house. "The prodigal has returned. Mom says she hardly sees you anymore. Come sit down. Dinner's ready."

"Where's Dad?"

Mom looked at Ruby, then to me, and shrugged. "He went to town and isn't back yet. Sometimes he doesn't get home until late."

"He's at the bar," Ruby said, "and you know it."

"Kelly's?" I said.

"In the past, I'd have raised Cain," Mom said, "but I don't have the heart to make his life harder. He doesn't know what to do with himself now there're no crops to plant or cows to milk."

I didn't remember Mother and Dad ever having harsh words. Even with that horrible cow business. Oh, Mother would nag now and then when Dad took a drink. She didn't like liquor; she thought it was the devil's brew. I suppose it was because she was raised a strict Methodist. I think our Methodist minister is a bit more forgiving. Not that he tolerates alcoholism, but he's reluctant to assign a man to hellfire. He's willing to give him a second chance—maybe even a third one.

"Catherine hasn't noticed his absences," Ruby said. "She has other things on her mind."

"Hush, Ruby. Catherine has helped. I don't know how we'd get along if Catherine and you didn't help with money, and Sharon and Ed let us stay in this house."

I felt guilty. Other than a few groceries, I had so little to give. "I feel so sorry for Dad. I wish I could help more."

Ruby shook her head. "That's his problem, having to live off his daughters. The more we do, the more he feels that he's failed us."

"Didn't Uncle Frank ask for help on his farm?" I said.

"He asked Dad to consider it," Mom said. "Dad said he wanted to think about it, but Ruby's right: Dad hates taking charity, although I think Uncle Frank needs the help."

"He has two hundred acres," Ruby said. "Most of it's tillable. Of course he needs the help."

"Let's eat," Mom said. "There's no use waiting for Dad. He'll have to eat leftovers—if he eats at all."

Ruby pulled chairs to the table. "Both of them are too old for the hard work," she said, "but hard work may be the therapy Dad needs right now."

"Life's so sad," I said. "Dad was the smartest in his family, but being smart isn't enough, it seems. Dad said his grandpa thought he'd fail."

"His grandpa never acknowledged your father's good qualities. Will's a good man, Catherine. He never raised a hand to me all these years, and he liked everyone, and they liked him, too. That's enough, Catherine. That's more than enough."

Mom didn't need to preach Dad's qualities. I hoped to find one as good.

We women ate supper alone tonight.

Dad came down for breakfast, drank a little coffee, and played with a piece of dry toast, but didn't take a bite. He put the toast down. "Girls … I don't … I'm … girls, I'm really sorry about last night. I wanted to be with you, but my intentions slipped through my fingers and fell into a glass of spirits. I'm ashamed." He lowered his head and placed his hands in his lap. After a moment, he looked up and turned to me. "I hardly ever see you anymore; you're so busy courtin'." Then a broad smile crossed his face. "Did I ever tell you about the time an old bullfrog saved my life when I was courtin', before I met your mother?"

Tense situations always reminded Dad of a story. Although we'd both heard it a half dozen times, Ruby said, "No, Dad, I don't think you did."

"Well, I'd visited Lenore—that was the girl I was dating at the time—and it got late, so I saddled my old brown gelding and rode cross-country toward our farm. There was no moon, and it was black as the inside of a cow's third stomach. I rode at a slow canter through marshlands that were unsuited for tilling or pasture, so I wasn't worried about fences. As I rode along, I could hear a bullfrog call, 'goround, goround, goround.' At first, I ignored his warning, but he persisted, 'goround, goround, goround.' So, figuring he knew something that I didn't, I took heed and went around. And it's a good thing I did. I found out the next day that the spring run-off had turned that lowland into a lake. If it wasn't for that bullfrog, I might have ridden right into it."

Ruby and I laughed. It wasn't the story but Dad's telling it that broke the tension.

Unlike Ruby, Dad was fond of Jonathon, and he must have known I was having a hard weekend. Dad studied me awhile, and then he said, "So your young man's away for a spell, now is he? I'd kind of hoped he'd be here to take me for a ride in his swift flying bug. I never dreamed I'd go so fast until the Lord gave me wings to fly to heaven." He gazed out the window into the sky. "I like your young man. Don't let him get away."

Ruby scowled.

At ten o'clock, we heard Ed's horn blare two beeps, the signal for us to get moving. We raced through the door and hopped into opposite sides of the old Ford's rumble seat.

Ed looked back at me. "It might not be as handsome as your beau's sportster, but it's an all-weather car. I don't have to stow it for winter."

I was determined not to discuss Jonathon today.

Ruby shouted. "It may be an all-weather car up there, but you'd be preaching a different sermon if you were back here."

I'd have thanked Ruby, but I knew she hadn't intended to defend Jonathon's pride and joy. She just loved to agitate Ed. But Ed was ready. "Well, Ruby, we can change places. If you don't like it back there, you're welcome to come up here and drive."

I heard Ruby's teeth grit. It was a continual annoyance that she couldn't drive anything that moved faster than a horse and buggy. "That'll change, Ed. One of these days, I'll drive your car."

"Now, now, children," Sharon said. "It's too nice a day to argue over the rumble seat. Why, Ruby, I'd love to sit back there if you'll change places. I like to feel the wind in my face."

"No, this will do fine. I'd not want to distract the driver. He has a hard enough time staying on the road without worrying about me. He'd probably forget to shout whoa at the stop signs."

Ed eyed the road for the rest of the drive toward Ashley Springs and the carnival.

"Did you hear that Buck the barnstormer is giving rides today," I said to Ruby, "and he'll only charge three dollars a person? I saw him in Madison, and he charged five."

"That's more than farmers will pay," Ruby said. "Buck knows his customers. I'll go if you will." Then before I could muster a reply, she shouted forward, "Hey Ed, are you flying today?"

Ed watched the road. Smart man.

Sharon leaned toward Ed. "Can we drive past Grandpa's old house after the carnival? I want to see it again. When we drive into Ashley Springs, it's like going home."

"We'll probably be too busy rushing the girls to the hospital."

"Ed, they'll not fly in that plane," Sharon said. "They'd no more fly than I would. They're too smart for that."

Ruby grinned like the Cheshire cat. I could feel one of her schemes building, and I couldn't for the life of me see how to get out of it.

"I miss Ashley Springs, too," I said. Better to have Ruby think about Ashley Springs. "It's a town with character, with resilience. The rock houses cling to the hillsides like nests on a cliff."

"It's the Cornish miners," Ed said. God bless him. "They built their homes with as much skill and care as they built shoring in their mines."

"Let's drive down the valley road on the way out of town," Sharon said. "I can picture the miners' wives as they stood in front of their cottages shaking their aprons at their husbands on the hill, telling them it was time to come home for supper. Can we stop at Pendarvis on the way home? Mom would love a Cornish pasty."

"I don't think they do carry-outs," Ed said.

"I wish I'd lived then," I said. "It was so romantic."

"Cathy, I wish you'd get romance out of your head," Ruby said. "The women worked like mules, and they weren't treated as good. Great-Grandpa was crushed in a tunnel collapse, and Grandpa went to Deadwood and never came back. How could you want a life like Grandma Tregonning—alone with five children and working for everyone in town?"

As usual, Ruby was right, but I wasn't about to give in. "Life was hard for everyone back then. Didn't Great-Great-Grandpa O'Shaughnessy travel thirty-five-hundred miles only to die of pneumonia ten miles from his new home? And he was a farmer."

Ruby huffed. "That's my point. He left Dad's great-grandma alone to raise ten kids in an alien land. Where's the romance in that?"

It did sound like a tragedy. It seemed as if our family's women always carried the load.

Two blocks from the fairgrounds, we heard the calliope hoot a syncopated rendition of "Double Eagle." Hotdog, cotton candy, and popcorn aromas teased our nostrils as we walked through the front gate. It was a grand carnival, straight from Chicago. We'd just entered the midway when a voice boomed, "Miss O'Shaughnessy, my guardian angel."

I turned in time to see Ruby's hand disappear into a hand of gnarled flesh. "Mr. Richter. How's that leg?"

The man stood as tall above me as a barn over a grain shed. And his ruddy face flashed a boyish smile.

"It's better than before I broke it, thanks to you and your nurses."

"And your son, Timmy, how's he doing?"

"I can't thank you enough for what you did for him. I'm afraid we'd not have him today if you hadn't stayed up nights with him. You'll never know. I can never … "

Then, to my surprise, this big farmer in fresh-boiled coveralls and a starched shirt looked ready to burst into tears. Over Ruby?

"Ben," she said, "I do the best I can, but I don't think Timmy would have made it without help from above. I want you to meet my family."

She introduced us, and one at a time, Ben thanked us for what Ruby had done. After he'd left, Ruby explained that a horse-drawn cart had tipped over on Ben and his son; how he'd gotten out from under the wagon and, from his knees, had lifted it with one hand while he pulled Timmy free with the other. Timmy had almost died, but the doctor, Ruby, and her nurses had saved him after a long battle against infection. I guess that I'd been so enveloped in my own life, I hadn't thought much about Ruby's job and how important her work is.

As we walked down the midway, carnies' promises sent tingles down my spine. I felt like a child again.

"Toss the ball into a bowl and take the goldfish home."

"Break a balloon and win a vanity set."

"Throw the ball in the basket and win this giant teddy bear."

"I'll guess your age or weight."

"Ring the bell and win a prize."

People walked away with a kazoo, Chinese handcuffs, a rub-on tattoo, or most likely, lighter pockets with nothing to show for the money spent. I'd learned long ago that it was a fool's errand to play these games, but I loved the excitement anyway—the incessant bantering, children begging, bells clanging, metal screeching, food smells, music, and laughter. A little girl cheered when her father won a barrette by plucking a duck from the stream. "I'll win you a goldfish, Maggie," a teenager said as his throws careened off the bowl's inverted rims. I saw a dandy slip a carny two dollars before his next throw won the China doll for his excited female companion. The movement, voices, and smells blended in a mixture that spelled carnival in capital letters.

Sharon's voice jolted me from my trancelike fascination. "Oh, Ed, win me a teddy bear. I always wanted one when I was little. Win me one—please?"

I couldn't believe that Sharon was so naïve as to think Ed could win a bear. Why, Ed couldn't hit an outhouse with a baseball unless he was throwing from the inside. And this game, tossing a ball into a bushel basket from about ten feet, was as rigged as any of them. As we watched other players, ball after ball bounced off the basket's bottom and out into space. No one could possibly win, it seemed.

I told Ed about the man who'd paid the carny two dollars, but he said, "I can't afford two dollars."

I didn't say he'd pay more than that before he'd win the bear. I think he knew.

Ed studied the other players as they unsuccessfully threw balls at the basket. Finally he stepped forward and paid the man his dime. I couldn't believe that prudent, thrifty man was throwing his money away, and my frugal sister had asked him to do it. It's no wonder that carnies thrived.

Ed placed his hand over the top of the ball and spun it toward the basket. The ball hit the bottom, jumped against the side, and slowly crawled over the rim—unlike others I'd watched that flew from the basket. Ed nodded at that, and I began to watch him more carefully. Ed paid once more. Again the ball slithered from the basket, even more slowly than the first time. Ed's third throw spun off the bottom, circled the basket once, twice, and then dropped back down.

"You won!" Sharon shouted. "You won me a teddy bear!" And then she did something I never thought I'd see; she threw her arms around Ed and gave him a kiss, on the lips, right there in front of all those people. It was so romantic. Sharon had a Prince Charming after all.

Ed turned bright crimson, and then he quickly pivoted toward the carny. "I'll take that dark brown bear, the one with the red ribbon around its neck."

The carny shook his head. "You broke the rules. No bear."

"What do you mean, I broke the rules? Your sign says the ball must be thrown underhand from behind the line. I stood behind the line and threw the ball underhand. I won a bear."

The carny grimaced. "Your hand crossed the line. No bear."

Sharon looked as if she'd wandered into a funeral home. "Don't I get a teddy bear?"

"Sorry, lady, but rules are rules. I can't give bears to everyone who breaks them. I'd go broke."

Then Ruby pushed Ed aside and walked up to the line. She stared the carny in the eye. "Lookit, mister, your sign says the ball must be thrown from behind this line." Ruby pointed down. "Most people would think that means to stand behind the line. My brother-in-law stood behind the line and threw the ball three times. You didn't say a word about rules when he missed twice, only when he won. You wrote your rule so you can deny a win. You're just a con man."

"Think what you like, Lady. Ain't nothing you can do."

"Oh, yeah?" Ruby looked across the midway to where Ben Richter stood beside the ice cream wagon. "Ben, come over here."

People began to pay attention as Ben ambled toward the stand. "Miss O'Shaughnessy, can I help?"

"Ben, this man's trying to cheat us. Tell him what we do to Chicago hucksters here in Wisconsin."

Ben glared down on the carny. "Hucksters? We don't have hucksters in Wisconsin. We chase them back to their kinfolk in Chicago." He said this simply, like he was discussing the weather, but his eyes never left the carny. "Sometimes they get there in one piece."

By now, attracted by Ben's booming voice, a crowd gathered around the tent. Ruby stepped across the line and behind the counter. She held out her hand. The carny tried to dodge around her. Ruby cut him off. He dropped his hands and looked into the crowd. With no help there, he turned back toward the shelf and grabbed the brown bear with the red ribbon. "Take it, lady, and leave me alone."

The crowd cheered. Sharon shrieked. "We won! I got my bear! Thank you, Ruby, thank you!"

Ruby handed Ed the bear, grasped his arm, and led him away. "Don't thank me. Thank Ed. He figured out how to win. I thought it was impossible. How'd you do it, Ed?"

This was another side of Ruby I hadn't seen for a while. Ruby embarrassed Ed at every opportunity, but fair is fair, and she knew he deserved better this time.

"I ... well, I watched the balls hit the bottom of the basket and fly over the rim. I could see that it acted like a spring and threw the balls back out." Ed handed the bear to Sharon who cradled it in her arms like a baby. "I remembered when I was young," he said. "I'd throw walnuts into a bushel basket so they wouldn't bounce out each time. I put back-spin on the ball, just like I did with those walnuts." He demonstrated the throw. "I didn't get enough spin until the third try, but it worked."

"You're a genius, Ed," Ruby said.

Sharon beamed as she hugged her bear. Ruby could anger a saint, but her heart was in the right place.

As we walked past the merry-go-round, children's squeals and exhortations for the horses to go faster stilled our progress and tickled our funny bones. I loved the gay music and colorful animals, but I knew these children would never feel the excitement of racing through a meadow with the wind in their faces. The only horse they'd know was one that waltzed in circles. I loved riding down the road beside Jonathon in his beautiful Bugatti, but even that could never replace the thrill of riding Lyda through the woods and fields and alongside the river.

The thought brought tears to my eyes for the children, and for me as well. I missed the farm.

Ed's voice jolted me back to the present. "Let's ride the Ferris wheel. From the top, we can see all over Ashley Springs."

Ed and Sharon grabbed the first seat because Sharon wanted the blue cab. Ruby and I hopped into the red one, right behind. As we began our ascent, Ed rocked their seat so that Sharon looked straight down. She screamed, and I heard her say, "If you do that again, Ed, I'll jump off this seat and pull you with me."

Ed behaved after that.

From the top, we could see across town in all directions. To the west, the Hinton road played footsie with Peddler's Creek, crossing back and forth twice within our sight. East across town, the zinc works stood out against the skyline, and as far south as we could see, gentle hills were pockmarked with black and white, brown and white, and black spots slowly grazing their way through the green grass. With each circle into the sky, we strained to see the lots that once held our old house, Grandpa's house, or the homestead my great-grandparents bought from Governor Dodge. But hills and trees thwarted efforts to make contact with our family's past. Steep ridges and a canopy of maples, oaks, and elms defended the town on all sides, while half a dozen steeples poked above the trees like giant pikes.

Below, people streamed into the carnival grounds, and those already inside looked like a mass of ants that scurried among vendors and around lines of people waiting to mount rides that spun, whirled, churned, or bucked them into a state of happy disorientation.

A bump—our seat lurched to and fro when the wheel stopped for a moment to let riders off. When it dropped another ten feet to let more riders exit, our seat swung violently once more. Each stop on the way down was signaled by Sharon's squeal, until our eight feet were back on ground.

"That's the last time I'm going higher than my kitchen step stool," Sharon said. "Ed, you scared the life out of me."

"I'm sorry, Sharon," Ed answered. "I didn't realize you were afraid of heights."

"I never used to be, but I guess I am now," Sharon said. "I bet I missed a great view, but I was too afraid to open my eyes. Did you see our house or Grandma's house?"

"It was disappointing," I said. "We weren't high enough to see through the trees to our houses."

"I bet we could see from the airplane," Ruby said. "Are you game, Catherine?"

Oh, no. I'd forgotten, and hoped she had, too.

She reached over and grabbed Ed's shoulder. "How about you, Ed? Do you have the gumption to leave the ground, or are you going to join Sharon on her step stool?"

"I'd better stay with Sharon until she calms down a bit."

"I thought so."

Ruby and Ed's relationship was back to normal.

"Well, Catherine, I guess it's you and me who have the backbones in this family. Are you ready?"

I wasn't sure that I had any of the spinal structure that Ruby valued, but I was intrigued. "Oh, okay, Ruby."

We walked to the field behind the carnival grounds where Buck's red-and-white-striped biplane sat tethered, surrounded by a small, admiring crowd. There were lots of lookers, but no takers. We'd not seen his plane in the air since we'd arrived that morning. We pushed through the onlookers to where Buck held court, describing the thrill of flying to one group while he shooed others who were intent on dissecting the innards of his grounded bird.

Ruby approached. "Buck, does this contraption really fly?"

"You better believe—" He turned away to confront two boys draped into the cockpit. "Hey, get away from there. That's not a Model T you're playing with." A swift kick to the pants sent one boy sprawling while the other dropped to the ground and hustled away. Buck turned his attention back to Ruby. "Does *Ellie* fly? She did three hours ago before these amateur mechanics worked her over. But I don't think they did much damage. Do you want a ride?"

Ruby said, "Yes," at exactly the same time I said, "No!"

Buck reached for my arm as I backed away. "Don't worry, she'll be fine. *Ellie* and I are under attack every time we attend one of these hick fairs."

Ruby scowled. "You don't mind taking this hick's money, do you?"

"Not at all, pretty lady. So there's no hard feelings, I'll double your flight to half an hour. How's that for a bargain? I assure you my *Ellie* will be safer up there than she is on the ground. I haven't paid for my trip down here yet. Will you lovely ladies help foot my bills? It'll be a ride you'll not forget."

Buck flew his hand through the air with thumb and little finger outstretched, adding a few loop-the-loops. "Haven't you ever looked into the sky and thought, 'I'd like to fly like a bird and look down and see a patchwork quilt of green, brown, and yellow fields and the houses, streets, and cars of a child's village.' It's only three dollars, the best bargain here."

"Is it really safe?" I asked.

"She's safe as a house wren and sings like a canary, honey. I assure you, she'll bring us back down from God's grand and glorious clear-blue sky."

"I never doubted we'd come down," Ruby said.

"Will we see our house through the trees?" I said.

"See your house? Dearie, I'll get so close you'll see the hearth down your chimney."

"That won't be necessary."

Ruby handed Buck six dollars and started to climb into the back cockpit. Buck grabbed her arm. "Whoa, girlie. That's where I sit. You're up front."

"Up front," I croaked. "Why are we up front? We'll get squished if we crash."

Buck jerked around. "I assure you, missy, you're just as safe in front as in back. This was an observation plane during the first war. Observers sat in front of the pilot where they could see better. You'll have the best view in town."

I nodded, but then had a thought. "Oh, good. What if a bird flies at us?"

"Just like on the ground, honey—duck."

Ruby and I crawled into the front cockpit and crowded together on a modified, narrow bench seat—behind the wind screen. Belts limited our movement, but there was plenty of foot room. Buck spun the propeller until the engine caught, and then he clambered into the cockpit behind us. As we taxied through the field, he shouted toward us. I could hardly hear him over the roar of the engine.

I shouted back, "What?"

"Thrills?" Ruby said. "He asked if we want thrills."

"Thrills—dives, loop-the-loops, figure eights," Buck said, louder this time.

I shook my head.

"No thrills," Ruby said, "just a nice ride over town."

We picked up speed and slowly peeled away from the ground. Buck circled over the city as he followed Highway 39 across town. We saw logs stacked for sawing and boards piled high at Nigel's Lumber Yard. The feed mill's silver storage bins, surrounded by burlap sacks, looked like metal buttons on a farmer's work shirt. We circled over High Street and looked down on the opera house, the library, and across town to the high school. I asked Buck to fly northwest to where I'd lived as a girl, and we soon soared over Grandpa and Grandma's house where we'd gathered for a grand Christmas feast. We swooped low over the house a second and third time before we curved away from town and flew over countryside tiled brown, green, and gold. I had to hand it to Ruby; it was grand, even better than galloping a horse across our meadow. We went everywhere—no trees or fences or buildings or rivers to stop us. I'd never felt so free. "I'm not frightened at all," I shouted at Ruby.

"This is pretty tame, isn't it?" Ruby said. "Don't you think we should try some of those thrills now?"

Deep in my reverie, I must have lost my mind. "Well, maybe. Yes, let's have some thrills."

Ruby strained her seatbelt as she twisted back toward Buck and shouted, "Mr. Buck, we'll have those thrills now!"

She'd no sooner said thrills than the bottom fell away from the plane. We dropped toward the earth like a falcon on its prey. As the plane went down, my heart jumped up, and my stomach grabbed hold of my liver and hung on for dear life, both meeting in my throat. I lost track of my heart as I concentrated on ridding my mouth of that bitter bilious taste.

But before I could swallow, the plane suddenly reversed into a steep upward climb, and the taste fell down my throat on its own. Ruby's face turned white, and we gasped for air. The plane imitated a roller coaster, then a racecar, before plunging, once more, off the high dive.

I couldn't catch my breath as the cyclone blew past. Self-preservation drove me to the only place in the cockpit void of wind, down below Ruby's dress, clinging to her ankles. She tried to join me, but the space was filled. She gasped for oxygen, dipped her head once more, then she waved toward Buck. "That … will be enough now!"

The plane banked hard right.

"Mr. Buck, that'll be enough thrills!"

The plane dropped from the sky.

"Mr. Buck, no more, no more thrills! We can go home now!"

I thought I heard laughter from behind.

"Buck, put this plane down!"

I felt the plane level off, drop a bit more, and then do a hippity-hop before it bounced violently and came to a stop.

I looked out from under Ruby's dress. "Are we down?"

The dress lifted and disappeared over the side.

I guessed that meant, yes, so I followed. As we walked away from the plane, I heard Buck mumble, "Country hicks."

Ed and Sharon ran to us as we staggered back toward the carnival. Sharon was as pale as Ruby. "I thought he was going to kill you, that nasty man."

Ed sidled over to Ruby. "How's your backbone holding up?"

Ruby kept walking.

Ed, a man of his word, did as he'd promised. He drove to Grandpa's house, and then up the hill to the lot where we used to live. But the house was no longer there. It had burned that tragic night. Our renter and his daughter died in the fire. Dad was accused of burning it down for the insurance, but that wasn't true. It was all so sad, but fortunately for us, we'd moved to the farm. The memories flowed like water from an artesian well.

"Remember Christmas at Grandma's?" Sharon said. "She cooked for days, and Grandpa butchered a huge Tom turkey."

"Grandma made the best apple pies," Ruby said. "Her crusts melted in your mouth. And we always had a plum pudding."

"What I remember most is her saffron bread," I said. "My friends thought it tasted like iodine, but I liked it. I guess you had to acquire a taste for it."

"Or have Cornwall in your blood," Ed said through puckered lips. "I never cared for it, but I'm no Cousin Jack."

"I remember mother's cakes," Sharon said. "She'd always bring an angel food for Christmas dessert. Everyone loved her angel foods."

"And she made them from scratch," I said. "She'd break thirteen eggs and use only the whites. Her angel foods were as light as a snowflake. We all begged her to make angel food birthday cakes."

"Until that awful mistake," Ruby said. "How could she possibly have gotten vanilla and liniment mixed up?"

We stopped the car in front of Grandpa's old eight-room house.

"Do you remember Grandpa moving the house up here after he bought it from Saint Mary's Parish?" I said.

"I was pretty young. I think I remember Dad and Uncle Frank with more horses than I'd ever seen before, but maybe I just remember the telling of it. I've heard the story so many times, I'm not sure."

"Will told me that after Grandpa bought the building from the parish, the old priest wouldn't let him move it from the grounds," Ed said. "I suppose he thought your grandpa would drop it off the foundation, and the parish would have to clean up the rubble."

"He should have thought about that before he sold it to Grandpa," Sharon said. "He didn't mind taking Grandpa's money."

"But Grandpa talked him into it," Ruby said.

"Cousin Joe told me that when Grandpa went to persuade Father McCrery, he took a quart of whisky along," I said.

"Now that's a detail Dad never mentioned," Sharon said.

Ruby rolled her eyes and shook her head. "You're not surprised, are you? You know he'd never tell us that."

I didn't say that Joe also told me that an hour later Grandpa and the Father stumbled arm-in-arm from the parish house singing "Sweet Molly Malone."

I missed Jonathon's singing. I missed Jonathon. I wondered if school business was his only interest that weekend.

18

IS DOING GOOD BAD?

Author's Note

The movie date I'll write about was a good way to show Catherine and Jonathon's relationship at a time when Catherine was questioning life—a way to show her ambivalence and Jonathon's steadfast strengths.

Mother told how one night when she was on a date with Carl they found and took a stray dog home. I borrowed that experience and included it as the ending to a night at the movies, a night in which Catherine's concerns about her father and Ruby were foremost on her mind.

Mother wrote in her book, "Because I had always wanted to get more education, that summer I went to the University of Wisconsin summer school in Madison. Before I started teaching, I did not have the money to go to school; now I had saved a little. The same summer, Carl went to school at Platteville Teachers College, thirty miles (from Ridgeway) in the opposite direction. On Friday night, he would drive to Madison in his convertible and pick me up at school and take me home to my folks in Ridgeway. He liked those trips with the wind blowing in his hair and me sitting beside him. He would sing songs like '*Girl of My Dreams, I love you, honest I do, you are so sweet,*' as well as other songs. I guess I knew he was special when one night he saw a stray dog along the road and stopped to pick it up and then took it home. At that moment, I knew he was a man after my own heart." (But the dog gnawed through its rope and ran away before the next morning.)

The ending didn't go according to plan, leading Mother to conclude, "Perhaps this was an omen predicting our future relationship. Although I didn't know it at the time, I was to bolt, too, when I began to feel too tied down."

Jonathon returned from Chicago, but he never said much about his interview, only that the current superintendent was having health problems and decided to retire in January, at the end of the first semester. Jonathon thought that he'd made a good impression, but he'd know more by the end of the year. When I pressed him about the likelihood of his being selected, he seemed ambivalent—said he wasn't sure he wanted the job. I wasn't sure whether that was to put me off or whether he was serious. Or maybe he didn't want to get his hopes too high. I tried to push doubts to the back of my mind. I was happy to have him back.

Small towns showed outdoor movies to keep the kids close to home and supervised. Sometimes the movie was ten or twenty years old, but for the kids who didn't have money, the price was right. The merchants paid the bill. And the movies brought parents to town for Saturday night shopping.

One weekend in late summer, Jonathon asked me to go with him to see *Faust*.

Jonathon sang that song, "The Good Old Summertime," as we rode along together.

I loved Jonathon's strong baritone voice. With him next to me, I felt secure, just like I'd always felt with Ruby. I joined in the chorus, ". . . strolling through the shady lanes / with your baby mine. ... "

I'd never been happier.

Jonathon reached for my hand. "Cathy, what more could I possibly want? You, my Bug, and a beautiful summer evening."

"Summer's almost gone, Jonathon. I don't want it to end. I'm not looking forward to winter."

"We'll spend the winter together planning for another summer of adventure in my blue Bug. Don't give up on me, Cathy."

"Just how many Wisconsin winters have you seen, city boy?"

Jonathon leaned back, pursed his lips, and raised an eyebrow. "Wisconsin winters? Just a stroll on the beach. Minnesota, now that's a real winter. And I didn't have you."

"Who did you have, Jonathon?"

"Cath—"

I laid a hand on his arm. "Oh, Jonathon. I shouldn't have."

He was stiff as a suit of armor. "No, you shouldn't. That's past."

We sat quietly. Why didn't I think before bringing up the past? I saw a glow on the horizon and knew we were approaching Mount Horeb. I'd not seen a movie on the green since grade school—Ashley Springs stopped showing them when a real theater came to town.

"Will we make it in time for the beginning?" I said. "I heard it's really scary. Maybe I'd rather be late."

"It's an old movie but a good one. I saw it when I was a teenager. Have you ever seen a Murnau movie? Did you see *Nosferatu*?"

"*Nosferatu*?"

"A vampire tale. Some loved it. Some hated it. I'm one of the loved-its."

"I'm glad I didn't see it. I hope this doesn't have vampires."

"We'll be there with time to spare."

"I'd never go to this alone."

"Well … I was hoping you'd want a shoulder to hide on."

It seemed that my slip about the past was forgotten. "Did you say his last film was *Nefarious*? Is this your nefarious scheme?"

***

As we walked back to the car, I squeezed Jonathon's arm. "How awful. It was wonderful."

He laughed.

"What?"

"Was it awful or wonderful?"

I slapped his arm, then I clenched tighter. "It was wonderfully made, but I'd never go again. I was scared to death."

"Are you glad you had my shoulder?"

"You are nefarious."

"But a nice nefarious, right?"

I clutched his arm and felt warm all over. "Yes, a nice nefarious. Oh, Jonathon, what a terrible dilemma. Faust had to give his soul to save his village, and Gretchen lost her baby in a snow bank."

"Did he have to, though?"

"He thought he did, but it didn't work. I don't think doing bad ever works."

"Oh? Would you steal food for starving children?"

"Steal? No—well, I don't know."

"It's not so easy, is it, Cathy? And Faust was an educated man, but he was faced with a life-and-death decision."

"I worry for Ruby."

"For Ruby?" Jonathon said. "I think you've left me behind."

"For her soul when she makes decisions about her patients."

"We face difficult decisions, too, about our students—"

"But it's not the same. Hers are life and death decisions. I don't know how she'll do it."

"Ruby's strong."

"That's why I'm afraid. How do you steel yourself when a life's at risk? Do you feel invincible?" I didn't like to think about it. "Maybe she'll sell her soul and not look back."

Jonathon patted and then squeezed my arm. "Don't worry about Ruby. She's a tough old girl."

He helped me into the Bugatti. While Jonathon maneuvered through the streets, he mumbled about the film's light and shadows producing a sense of dread when Mephisto flew over the city. My mind was elsewhere. I thought about Faust and Ruby. What if she'd make a wrong decision, one she'd have to live with the rest of her life?

"Evil permeated every pore of your body," he said. "Couldn't you just feel it?"

That got my attention. "I'm sorry?"

"Cathy, aren't you listening?"

I shuddered. "I hated Mephisto."

Jonathon twisted toward me. "Of course, we all hate the devil. It's just his pleasures we like."

"Don't mock me, Jonathon."

"I'm sorry, Cathy, but it's true. Take Faust. His temporary contract became permanent because he couldn't resist carnal satisfaction."

"I worry about Dad. Evil is a dangerous bedfellow." I wished we'd not come to this movie.

"Your dad?"

"He drank a little at times, but … now … he's drinking more."

Jonathon took my hand as he drove at a slow pace for home. "Will's a good man. He'll be okay once he gets back on his feet."

"I hope so, but I don't know. Mother nagged him for his nips, but now it's gotten serious, she's backed off."

"Something will show up—have patience with him, Cathy."

I pounded my fist on the dash. "I hate the devil and his vices."

"Well, yes, but … it wasn't Mephisto who started the trouble."

"What do you mean, it wasn't Mephisto?"

"If Faust hadn't burned his books, he'd not have conjured up Mephisto. It was the book burnings. Destroying books never leads to anything good."

"You're a silly man."

"Only a little, my dear Cathy. Just a little."

"They died in each other's arms. Wasn't that romantic?"

"I'd say, tragic."

I sighed. "But love won out. The devil was banished."

"Liebe conquers all. I still say it was tragic."

We drove west from Mount Horeb. We were almost to Barneveld when we saw an animal alongside the road. Jonathon stomped his brakes and veered right until his headlights illuminated a dog struggling to free itself from a barbed-wire fence. He drove onto the shoulder, jumped out, and ran towards it.

"Be careful, Jonathon," I shouted after him, "he may be rabid."

We walked closer and could see that the dog was attached to a rope that had become tangled in the fence. He was bloodied and crouched and trembled as we approached.

"Go slow," Jonathon said as he knelt about ten paces away. I dropped down beside him, and we watched for a while.

"He doesn't look rabid," I said. "He's not aggressive or foaming at the mouth. He's just a frightened mutt."

"Hush now, boy. Stay calm. We won't hurt you," Jonathon said softly. He reached back for my hand. "He's as gaunt as a stray in the desert. He's either wandering or been mistreated."

"We've gotta untangle him from the fence, or he won't last long. What will we do with him?"

The mutt strained against the rope.

Jonathon eased forward and talked softly all the time. He reached in his trousers' pocket, pulled out a penknife, and tossed it at my feet. "Wait until I get to him, then cut the rope. I'll grab it."

"Be careful, Jonathon. He might bite."

"I think he knows we're helping."

Jonathon approached with one hand extended toward the mutt's nose. The dog sniffed and whimpered loudly. Jonathon continued his soft, comforting chatter and began to pet the mutt's head. I almost cried at his gentleness. I wanted to reach out and hug him.

He nodded to me. I eased forward, pulled open his tiny knife, and sawed through the rope.

Jonathon grabbed the freed strand but let it hang loose so the mutt would no longer feel restrained. At first, he lunged away, but before reaching the end of the rope, he circled back and lay at Jonathon's feet. Jonathon continued to talk softly and pet the animal.

"What do we do with him?" I said. "Should we let him go?"

"He looks terrible. I say take him home and feed him. There's water in the car."

I hesitated. "What if he belongs to someone? Are we stealing?"

"Ah, another Faustian dilemma, my dear. Are we doing bad by doing good? Is taking him our pact with the devil?"

Why was life so complicated?

Jonathon tugged the rope and urged the mutt along. "I'll ease your conscience, my sweet, and make a deal with you. We'll take him home tonight, but tomorrow morning I'll drive to Sheriff Schroeder's office."

"He'll shoot him."

"Not if I can help it. If he can't find the owner, I'll take the dog and care for him. How's that?"

I shivered as I walked toward the car.

The mutt drank a canteen of water without taking a breath. He'd been there awhile.

"That'll hold him until we get home," Jonathon said. "I hope he can hold it, too."

Jonathon spread his jacket on the inner edge of my seat, picked the filthy mutt up, and looked toward me as he set him down. "This might be a bit tight for you, but it's only a short drive to home."

I snatched the jacket away. What was he thinking? "Jonathon, that's a brand new jacket. He'll ruin it."

Jonathon took it from me and placed it back down. "Cathy, it's easier to clean my jacket than you or the Bugatti. Just curl the outer edge over your legs so it'll keep you from getting dirty. It'll be okay."

The mutt settled into the jacket like a brood hen on her nest. I scratched his ears and neck all the way home. He raised his head for the first time when Jonathon stepped from the car, but he never moved from the jacket. Jonathon walked me to my door, took me in his arms, and convinced me that he'd seen too many Clark Gable movies. "It's been a glorious summer, each day more wonderful than the last," he said. "May I come by after church tomorrow? Let's pack a picnic and drive to Blue Mounds."

"Jonathon, what about the mutt?"

"Let him get his own girl."

"Oh, Jonathon!"

I didn't know which I liked best, his tenderness or his teasing.

"I'll take him to Sheriff Shroeder, first thing in the morning."

"You promise?"

"I hope they find his owner. I think I'd come in second if I had to compete for your affection."

I heard a yip as Jonathon got back in the car.

I awoke in the middle of the night after pulling babies from snow banks and fighting a seducer who looked like a slicked-up Jonathon. I was exhausted from the devil's exhortations. Darkness tiptoed toward morning's light.

The next morning, Jonathon's Bugatti roared down Main Street just as people streamed from their churches. Children ran behind and shouted, "Mr. Hays! Mr. Hays!" Parents shook their heads and said, "Doesn't he know it's the Sabbath?"

I ran out the door and raced down the street toward home. I heard the roar of the Bugatti behind me as I ran into the house, changed to traveling clothes, and loaded the picnic basket with sandwiches, utensils, canned food, and fruit from the ice box.

I jumped into the car. "What about the mutt?"

Jonathon looked glum. "I lost him."

"You lost him! How could you lose him?"

"I'm sorry, Cathy. I took him home, fed him, and tied him out. I even put a blanket down for him. But he was gone this morning—chewed the rope."

"Oh, Jonathon. All that worry, and he's no better off than last night. What's the good of it? Did we make any difference at all?"

"He's not tangled in a fence. He has a chance. Can we ask for more?"

"I had terrible dreams last night about Gretchen. The world turned its back in her moment of need."

"We didn't turn our back on mutt."

"And it did no good. Her baby would have died anyway." I hung my head, suddenly overwhelmed by it all. "Do we ever make a difference?"

"Ruby must think we make a difference," Jonathon said, "or she wouldn't be a nurse."

"Ruby doesn't count. She's different."

"What do you mean, different?"

"She'd know what to do. I wouldn't. Maybe she'd have saved the baby."

"Cathy, don't be foolish. If she could have saved the baby, it's because she's trained for it. Maybe she can save babies, but you save minds. That's just as important."

"I don't know."

"Don't be down, Cathy. You can't be Ruby's little sister forever. You're just as smart." Jonathon reached over and gently poked my side. "And a whole lot prettier."

I blushed and giggled. "Do you think flattery will get you anywhere?"

"I sure hope so."

I reddened further as Jonathon reached for my hand and began to sing the words to "In the Good Old Summertime."

I was affected more than I could know by that night's experience. That was the first time I'd thought of myself as equal to Ruby. I hadn't thought of teaching being as important as Ruby's job, and I liked Jonathon's assertion that I was a whole lot prettier. Maybe those thoughts were the impetus that turned my next meeting with Ruby in a different direction. Maybe they stiffened my spine more than I thought possible.

19

CATHERINE REBELS

Author's Note

In this next action scene, I've brought Ruby and Catherine's disagreement over Jonathon to a fever pitch. Catherine shows spunk and turns on her sister—professing her love for Jonathon and accusing Ruby of being jealous, mean-spirited, and spiteful.

I was deep in thought while walking home late in the evening when a spectacle in the western sky wrenched me from my reverie. High-up, angry, blackish-blue clouds were tinted with bright orange and red streaks, but on the horizon the bright yellow orb, refusing to yield the day without battle, shot darts of red, orange, and yellow into its nightly adversary. I imagined a war in the western sky, a clash between day and night.

A shiver crept down my spine. I hoped the battle on the far horizon didn't portend conflict of a different kind. Ruby would be home this weekend.

Mom told me that Dad had stopped going to Kelly's Bar, so I wasn't surprised that he was there when I got home. And he was his old self, joking and teasing the whole evening. It seems that he was cooking up some deal with Gusta, but he didn't talk much about it that night. We learned more about it later. But I could see he was keyed up.

At first Ruby and I were so busy helping Mother place supper on the table that we hardly spoke to each other.

After dinner, Dad continued his Irish banter and stories for a while, but eventually he wound down, and we all went off to bed. Ruby and I still shared a room after all these years. She hadn't mentioned Jonathon during dinner, but I knew that would change. Ruby didn't give up easily. But I was determined not to be cowed by my older sister this time. I thought I was ready when she said, "Catherine, do you think it's good to spend so much time with Jonathon? Why, you don't really know him, do you?"

I had steeled myself for this moment, but, once again, I began to wither under Ruby's assault. Why did she have to make something so good feel so bad? My stomach churned, and my throat burned. I started to walk away.

But I knew this was the time to stand up to Ruby. I turned back. "I love my time with Jonathon. He's kind and sweet and funny and gentle. He's everything I've ever wanted in a man. He makes me feel tingly and happy when I'm with him. He makes me feel like a woman. I'd be with him now if I could. I love him."

"You're infatuated with him. You've never had an adult boyfriend, and you hardly know him. He's suave and sophisticated. You're just a naïve little farm girl, and he's swept you off your old gray mare and whisked you away in his sky-blue Bugatti." She took my hand, but I pulled away. "He may seem like your Prince Charming, but this is no fairy tale. This is real life, and in real life, you don't always live happily ever after."

And that was the moment I hated her. My sister. My protector and confidant. My dearest friend. The person I had loved more than any other. I hated her. I did want to live happily ever after, and I would, no matter what she said. I felt all this building inside me until I couldn't hold it back. "You're mean, Ruby. You're jealous because you don't have a Prince Charming, and you never will. You'll chase him away with your analytical high-handedness. You'll dissect him until his beauty turns to ugliness and his heart bleeds. You don't want me to be happy because you can't be happy. Misery likes company."

I fell to the floor and sobbed.

Ruby bent and put her arms around me. "Cathy, I don't want you hurt, and I don't want us to fight either. Let's enjoy our time together this weekend. Truce? Can we declare a truce?"

I didn't feel like fighting, but I didn't feel like a truce either. I was numb. I wanted Jonathon.

20

CATHERINE STANDS HER GROUND

Author's Note

To my knowledge, Mother did not have interactions with Carl's parents, nor did she suggest that Carl had the prior experiences with a lover that's described in this story. But this was an opportunity for me to extend the story line and to illustrate the independence and confidence that Catherine was beginning to show.

Ruby and I got through the weekend without further disputes, but we avoided mentioning Jonathon. I was thrilled when I saw Jonathon Sunday night and he proposed an outing for our next weekend together.

Today I'd meet Jonathon's father, a professor, and I was nervous as a cat in a calf pen as I rode alongside Jonathon in his Bugatti. The day was hotter than Hades, and the air vibrated with heat that radiated off the fields. We chased dust devils down the road as we roared along with Bugatti's top down, which made up for the absence of air conditioning in the car. Farmers stopped their work to mop their brows, but the wind that fanned our hair and faces cooled us like ice cools a glass of tepid tap water.

"I never knew a drive could feel so good!" I shouted to Jonathon over the rushing wind."

"Nothing's cooler than racing along inside a convertible in summer. Well, maybe a motorcycle, but they're not for me."

"Ah, but you've never ridden a horse. Riding Lyda bareback down the lane and through the meadows was real freedom. No roads to demand I circle a hill or view streams from afar."

Jonathon stepped on the accelerator. The Bug zoomed forward. "Lyda couldn't move like this."

"She didn't feel any slower. A gallop turned my blouse and tresses back towards home. We'd outrace the dust off her hooves, and tall weeds would slap my legs red. I miss the farm, Jonathon. I didn't want to grow up. I didn't want to leave."

Jonathon took my hand. "I'm glad you grew up, and I'm glad you're still a country girl, too."

Suddenly, Jonathon braked hard for a deer that scampered across the road in front of us, throwing me against the dashboard.

He grabbed my arm and pulled me back. "Are you hurt, Cathy?"

"I'm okay, thanks to your padded dash." I watched the deer race away. "Look at that beautiful animal. I hate to see them dead on the road. I never ran an animal down while riding a horse."

"That's the price of progress."

"Progress? Lots of changes and they're all called progress, but I'm not so sure."

We continued toward Ashley Springs, but at a less frenzied pace. Jonathon hummed a familiar song as we cruised along. When he got to the chorus lines, we sang together, his baritone and my alto. "If you knew Suzie, like I know Suzie, oh, oh, oh what a gal."

We often sang as we rode, and I must say, we sounded pretty good.

After half a dozen choruses, it petered out.

Jonathon squeezed my hand. "It's not Suzie, but Cathy that I dream about. From now on it's, 'If you knew Cathy, like I know Cathy, oh, oh, oh what a gal.' Don't forget, now."

"It's you who'll forget. I see all those students and young teachers mooning around you. And I hear all the rumors. I try not to listen."

"You better not listen. They're just that: rumors."

Jonathon retreated back into himself and was silent as we drove the last mile into Ashley Springs. But I couldn't get those letters tied with the red ribbon off my mind. Why couldn't I let it be?

"We'll be just in time," I said. "They're expecting us at noon, aren't they?"

"Dad'll be at the table whether we are or not." He seemed relaxed again, more like his old self. "It's just around the corner."

"I've never eaten with a professor before." My stomach began to churn. "I hope he doesn't think I'm a country hick."

Jonathon looked over and raised an eyebrow. "Why would he think that?"

I hunkered into my seat. "Because I am."

"Well, professors are a strange tribe on the whole, and he is a bit pompous. But I've seen gravy on his tie more than once, so it's hard to take him too seriously." He mussed my hair, already blowing free in the wind. "You'll be just fine. He's not a bad sort once you get to know him. Don't worry."

But I did.

The meal ended in a draw; I didn't misuse my salad fork, and Dr. Hays didn't spill anything on his tie. The food was a tad different than the country fare I was accustomed to, but good enough. I thought the hors d'oeuvres were tasty, although the farm kids I knew would have likened them to sucking a sweet clover bud—just a little flavor burst.

After coffee was served, Dr. Hays stood. "Ladies, if you'll excuse us, I'd like to show Jonathon my new toy." He took Jonathon's shoulder. "I'll get around these hills now."

"What's it this time, Dad? A new Schwinn?"

"Oh, better than that. Come and see."

Dr. Hays called to us as they headed toward the door. "We'll be back by the time you ladies finish the dishes."

Jonathon shrugged and followed his father but turned to his mother as he stepped over the threshold. "Be gentle with her, Mom. Don't tell too many secrets."

"Secrets?" Mrs. Hays said. "I don't know any secrets." She shrugged her shoulders toward me. "Miss O'Shaughnessy, I—"

"Just, Catherine, please."

"That's a deal, if you'll call me Dorothy."

"It's a deal, then."

Dorothy seemed to want to talk, to tell her story, and I was happy to listen. "After Charles retired from the university, we weren't sure what to do," she said. "He wanted to stay in the city. He liked coffee with his cronies, the theatre, the museums." She sighed. "I liked them, too. But then my sister, who lived alone in this house, died. This was my parents' home after they moved from the farm."

"What were their names?"

"You lived in Ashley Springs as a girl, didn't you? You might have known them. Wandsfield. Tim and Chris Wandsfield. They ran the Ashley Springs bakery."

"Sure, I knew of it."

"Well, when Sarah died, we had to make a decision—either sell the house or live in it. We'd visited often when my parents had lived here, but less after they'd died."

She took my arm and led me to the kitchen table. Clearly, she'd persuaded her husband to join her here. I liked this woman.

"I grew up outside of town," she said, "so Ashley Springs felt like home. Charles loved it, too. For a geologist, this Driftless Region is the mother lode." Dorothy motioned to a straight-backed chair. "Please sit down while I do the dishes."

"We'll be done quicker if I dry."

"You're a guest. You shouldn't work."

"But I want to. I do them at home. We can talk while we work."

"I see why Jonathon likes you so much."

I felt warm all over, and my face was hot. Why did that thought fluster me so?

"I don't want to rush things, but I know my son. I can tell that he cares very much. Catherine, I like you, too. I do hope it works out … this time."

"Um … this time?"

"Jonathon didn't tell you about Helen?" She put a hand to her mouth. "Oh, dear, I guess I do have secrets."

"Dorothy, you don't —"

"No, no, it's … They're not guilty secrets, and I'm sure Jonathon would have told you in time. When he was ready, I mean."

"Is it … I think you'd better tell me now."

"Yes, well, they were going to be married, and then two years ago, she died in that horrible accident."

"How awful."

"Jonathon was principal of the newest school in Minneapolis. Afterwards, he left and came down here to little Logan Junction." She ran more hot water into the sink. "It was a surprise to Charles and me, especially Charles. He expected Jonathon to become superintendent of the Minneapolis schools someday, and maybe join the university."

"Jonathon never said—"

"No, he never talks about it, not even to us. He holds it in." She shook her head. "It's not good."

"I'm so sorry."

"Well, I think you're the best medicine for what ails him. Let's get these dishes done."

As we finished, there was a mechanical sputtering and then a roar from the shed out back. It died out almost immediately.

Dorothy glanced toward the noise. "They may be there a while. Why don't we have tea in the parlor while we wait?"

I agreed. I wanted to know more about the mysterious Helen. But by the time tea was served, I decided maybe I didn't, so I changed the subject. "Jonathon and his father seem pretty close."

"Yes and no. They were close while Jonathon was growing up—our youngest boy, you know. But I'm not sure now."

"Because Jonathon left Minneapolis?"

"That, and Helen. But it started long before, back when Jonathon was in his second year of college. His brother, Edward, was killed in Italy."

"I didn't know." I was surprised that Jonathon had never mentioned a brother or a fiancée. Were there other things he hadn't told me?

"We were all devastated," Dorothy said. "But most of all Jonathon. Edward was two years older, but they did everything together. Mostly baseball. First in high school, then in summer league."

"Jonathon still loves the game," I said.

"Although Jonathon was younger, he was the better athlete, and Edward knew it. In high school, he'd tell Jonathon, 'You'll be a major leaguer someday, and I'll watch all your games.'" Dorothy poured hot water and handed me the box of teabags. "Jonathon was offered a contract to play minor league ball for the Cubs. He was still deciding when that terrible letter came."

"How awful."

"Charles wanted Jonathon to finish university, to get a college education. He thought professional ballplayers were like grown-up children. He'd say, 'They don't call the Dodgers bums for nothing.'"

"So he didn't play?"

"No. He'd gotten a deferment from the draft because he was a good student, and he'd taken ROTC his freshman year. He planned to enter service as soon as he graduated. After the letter, he forgot about baseball. He forgot about school. He only thought about one thing—avenging Edward."

"He never mentioned service, either."

"He didn't go. Charles finally convinced him to stay in college. He said that we couldn't bear to lose two sons. By the time he graduated, the war was over. I don't think Jonathon ever forgave his dad."

"He didn't want to play ball anymore?" I knew how much Jonathon loved baseball.

"No. I think Edward was the main reason he considered playing professionally. Without a big brother to be proud of him, he had no interest in pursuing the sport."

"But he did what his father wanted."

"It was probably best. He was a fine scholar, and I've heard that professional athletes do live vagabond lives."

We heard the men laughing at the door. "Dad, you really did it this time. You're going to kill yourself." Jonathon looked toward me. "Do you know what Dad did now? He went and bought an Indian."

"He—pardon me?"

"An Indian motorcycle. He bought a motorcycle. Mom, how could you let him? He'll kill himself."

"Let him," Dorothy scowled. "When did he ever ask my permission?"

Dr. Hays grimaced. "Enough, you two. We've got company. Maybe I'll go out and start it each day. I love the sound of its power."

"I'm sure you do, Dad. I'm sure you do."

"If I could afford it," I said, "I'd have one. I wouldn't be bound to the road." My imagination shifted to high gear. "I'd go over the hills, up the streams, just like on horseback."

"Better, Catherine, better," Dr. Hays said, "I don't have to feed it, rub it down, or clean stalls. With a little gasoline, I can go all day."

My enthusiasm spun out of control. "I'd ride to Castle Rock, down the Pecatonica, maybe all the way to Illinois," I said. "Over the bluffs to the Wisconsin River, to the Mississippi."

Everyone went silent, and I could feel myself turning red.

"We can go there in my convertible," Jonathon said. "And we will Catherine, we will."

Dr. Hays cleared his throat. "Yes, I think riding in Jonathon's convertible would be the proper way to see the world—for a young lady, that is."

"Remember, Charles, Catherine isn't one of your brittle little university coeds," Dorothy said. "She grew up on horseback, just like I did. A motorcycle isn't such a stretch."

"I suppose not. And Catherine does seem to harbor an appreciation for why I bought the Indian. I thought it'd be a grand machine for riding out to find specimens in the Coulee Region. I've studied and taught coulee geology for most of my life. You do know what the Coulee Region is, don't you, Catherine?"

I couldn't believe his arrogance. "My dear professor, I've lived here all my life. I teach it to my eighth-graders. Of course, we study it by its correct name, the Driftless Region."

"Yes, that's right, the Driftless Region. But most people know it by its colloquial name, the Coulee Region."

"Of course, from the French word *couler*, meaning to flow, like through a valley. Still, I expect my eighth-graders to learn the correct terminology."

Professor Hays glared at me a moment, then his lips eased into a smile. "Yes, yes. Jonathon, you've got a remarkable young woman here. I wouldn't have believed that she grew up on a farm."

I was surprised he hadn't said backwoods, wilds, or boondocks. "Dr. Hays, some of our young people, mostly the boys, never get past eighth grade. But to get an eighth-grade diploma, they have to pass a test that would be difficult for your fine city students."

Dr. Hays looked from Jonathon to his wife, but neither stepped in to help with this feisty, young farm hick. Ruby would be proud of me.

"Well, yes, I suppose. I didn't mean—My dear, can we call a truce? We can agree that this area is more beautiful than any place in Wisconsin, can't we?"

"I'm sorry for getting on my high horse, but I'm a little sensitive about the failures of country folks right now." I lowered my head. If Dr. Hays was like other professors I'd known, he'd love to profess, even more so if I asked his opinion. "I must sound as if I know it all, but I don't. I never learned why the great ice masses missed this part of Wisconsin. Was it just luck, divine providence, or what?"

"I'm not sure about the involvement of the divine, but if the intent was to shelter this area from that rampaging, raging, ripping ice mass, the plan was perfect. To the north of us is a highland, to the east and west, lowlands. When the south-flowing ice mass hit the highland, it slowed, but continued through the lowlands, only to rejoin to the south of us, leaving this area an island surrounded by ice. Before there was time for the ice from the north, east, west, and south to fill the void, the glacier began its retreat, leaving about fifteen thousand square miles untouched. It's almost all in southwest Wisconsin, but some is in Minnesota, Iowa, and Illinois."

I flashed my most demure smile. "Thank you for that geology lesson, Dr. Hays. I feel like a student in one of your classes."

"I wish you would've been. I think you'd have been … what do the kids say? 'The cat's meow?' But on second thought, my self-esteem might never have recovered. Would you like to see the Indian?"

"I would, thank you."

We traipsed outside to where he kept his cycle, all except Dorothy, who'd said, "I'll stay in the house. It's too hot out there to suit me. I think I'll hear more from that machine than I want before the summer is through."

Dr. Hays unlocked the shed door, and there it stood—his slick, red cycle with the word Indian prominently displayed across its tank. As he wheeled it into the sunlight, bursts of crimson exploded from its surface like reflections off a ruby. My fondness for horses began to weaken.

"It's beautiful, Dr. Hays. I'd sure like to ride through the country with you sometime."

"I'd take you for a ride now, except I think it'd be wise to practice a bit before putting anyone at risk."

I looked at Jonathon, who shrugged his shoulders. "Don't look at me. I've never ridden one. I'm happy with my Bugatti. Speaking of riding, I think it's time we hit the road."

We re-entered the house to say goodbye to Dorothy. As Dr. Hays and Jonathon headed to the front door, I thanked her for the meal and her kind hospitality.

She took my hands in hers and pulled me forward with a big hug. "Catherine, you can't know how much I've enjoyed meeting you. You so remind me of myself at your age." She stepped back. "Our life has been so different these last thirty years that I'd almost forgotten, but it's a good memory. After today, I'm not sure Charles will ever be the same. But he likes you. I can tell that."

"I did enjoy our time together."

I rushed to catch the men at the car. "Jonathon, can we drive home through Hinton? It's only a little further, and the valley is so beautiful this time of year, so lush and green."

As we drove off, Dr. Hays waved and shouted, "Catherine, come back again after I've mastered the Indian."

"I'm not sure Dad knows what to do with you. He's not used to being challenged in his areas of expertise, certainly not by a woman." Jonathon took my hand. "But he liked you. I can tell you that."

I could see that Jonathon thought like his mother. And I liked that.

I was glad to have met Mr. and Mrs. Hays, but his father's lecture exhausted me. I wasn't about to tell him that I knew all that before. I'd read Lawrence Martin's *Physical Geography of Wisconsin*, but I hadn't wanted to damage his ego further. After all, he was Jonathon's father.

But I was proud of myself. Long after, I decided that was the day that frayed the strings that had bound me so long. That was the day I felt like a whole person. I was ready to face the world.

21

THE BEGINNING OF THE END

Author's Note
After Mother started school in Madison, she didn't see Carl as often because of the distance between them, and they began to drift apart.

Mother knew that Carl wanted to move to a large school district, so when the letter came offering him the job, she wasn't surprised. Her stomach churned, and she sensed what it was when he told her he'd received a letter.

Mother wrote, "He got a job in Hammond, Indiana, that he wanted and was soon gone, although he did write to me from Hammond. Soon after we said good-bye, he sent a letter in which he said, 'You were standing in the doorway as I was ready to get in my car. I looked back and saw you standing there and just wanted to come back and take you in my arms.' I never saw nor heard from him for a long time after that. I guess there were reasons why I was never too sure it would work for us. I always thought that he was so much above me. I thought that I could never fit into his life as administrator of a big school system, because I was not outgoing or self-confident as I should have been. Perhaps neither of us would have been happy."

As eager as I was to face the world, I could no longer do it on the pittance of a salary I was making as a country school teacher. That's why I decided to take a job in Madison that fall, working for the Wisconsin Department of Transportation in the Division of Motor Vehicles. It wasn't the most exciting job, but it paid a higher wage and provided me with twelve full months of salary.

Jonathon drove to see me each Friday evening through the fall and early winter. He'd pick me up when I left work, and we'd drive to the University Union where we'd grab a bite to eat before attending a movie or a play. Sometimes the Union had musical entertainment, and we'd stay and listen to the bands perform. I still remember the songs we danced to: "Elmer's Tune," "Almost Like Being in Love," and "In the Mood." We loved dancing to "In the Mood." We could dance the swing with the best of them. And before the evening was over, Jonathon always requested, "In the Good Old Summertime." That was his favorite song.

After a tedious day sorting license plate applications and car registrations, I was exhausted by the time we stepped into the car for the drive back to Logan Junction, but Jonathon always seemed to be fresh and alert. Although I was half-asleep, I felt comfortable and safe with my head on his shoulder. On those nights, I knew I loved this man.

I helped Mother when she needed me, but no longer having papers to grade or lessons to write, I spent most of my weekends with Jonathon. Although it lingered on the edge of my thoughts, I avoided asking him about Chicago and he hadn't mentioned it either. I think both of us feared that these wonderful days might end.

Before we knew it, it was Thanksgiving. It was as warm and sunny as a day in late spring. We were all together for the first time in months—Mother and Dad, Sharon and Ed, and Ruby came home, too. Everyone was happy and congenial, seeming to reflect the warmth of the day. What a relief! I had been worried that Ruby might start giving Jonathon the third degree about his past, or perhaps get snippy with him or ignore him completely. But she was as sweet as the honey on a Southern cured ham. If anything, she was a little too sweet, but I was happy for that instead of hostility. I couldn't have known it then, but that would be the last time we all sat down for a meal together.

After we'd finished eating Mother's humongous Thanksgiving meal, Jonathon took my hand and said, "Cathy, it's so nice outside. Let's take a walk."

I was excited to be alone with him at first, but his voice sounded strained, his fingers tightly clenched mine, and he didn't smile like he usually did when I looked into his eyes. I could tell something was troubling him, but I wasn't sure I wanted to know what it was. I remained quiet as we walked together in the direction of his school. We reached the school building, and he motioned toward a bench alongside the entryway.

"Let's sit for a while," he suggested.

We sat there, still not talking, until I finally got up enough courage to ask, "Jonathon, what's wrong?"

He looked down at me and forced a pinched smile. "I hope nothing, Cathy."

"What is it?" Deep down, I feared what his answer would be. I hoped I didn't sound as desperate as I felt.

"I received a letter from Chicago last week. They want me to fill their school superintendent's opening starting in January."

I coughed to clear the lump from my throat. "Oh, Jonathon, this is what you've always wanted." I hated to say it, but I knew I must. "This is your big chance. You've got to take it."

I didn't anticipate his next words.

"Cathy, I want you to come with me."

Was this a proposal? I wasn't ready—not yet anyhow.

"Cathy, I know you don't like big cities, but we'd be together, and there're so many things we could enjoy there."

I didn't know what to say. Could I leave my beloved woodlands, fields, and family to start a new life in a world of concrete—a place of bustling streets and high-rise buildings where people literally lived on top of each other? I had already had a taste of city life in Madison, but I only regarded Madison as a place that I worked until I could get back to my real home on the weekends. In actuality, Iowa County was much more than a home. It was my universe. It was a place that seemed untouched by the passage of time, which allowed me to keep my memories of Ruby, Sharon, Dad, Mother, Gusta, Petr, Mabel, Lyda, Fanny Too, and the Jenkins boys as fresh as the berries that grew every year on my beloved bluff.

Everything I had ever wanted or needed was right there in Iowa County—everything, that is, except for a future with Jonathon. Every time I crossed the county line, I felt like I was leaving a little piece of myself behind. It seemed so cruel, to have to choose between the man I loved and everything else that was important to me. I knew what Ruby would tell me—that Jonathon had secrets and I'd regret giving him my trust—but that was something I didn't want to think about.

Finally, I answered, "Jonathon, I want to be with you, but I need time to think about it."

And that's all I did for the next few weeks—think about it night and day. Jonathon and I continued to see each other, but it seemed different now that such a big decision weighed heavily on my mind.

Although Jonathon frequently gave me an imploring look, as if he was trying to squeegee an answer through my lips, he didn't ask the question again. And I couldn't give an answer. I was exhausted wrestling night and day with the biggest decision of my life. Although I wanted to be with Jonathon, I felt just as strongly that I couldn't leave Iowa County and the family that I loved so dearly.

And then there was Helen—Jonathon's mysterious fiancée who died under such tragic circumstances. Jonathon never talked about her, and I never brought her up, but she always lingered at the edge of my mind. Funny how a woman whom I had never met could fuel my doubts about whether I should be with the man that I loved.

Jonathon helped alleviate those doubts by being kind and patient with me. A lesser man might have been offended that I hadn't immediately agreed to drop everything in my life so I could move with him to Chicago, but not Jonathon. He understood completely what I was going through.

One night in mid-December, we were sitting together in his winter-weather Ford Sedan Coupe, and he brought up the subject of Chicago. He told me he would be leaving right after Christmas so he could get settled in before the new semester begins. "I want to be with you, Cathy, but not unless you're sure you want to be with me," he said.

I thought this was my cue to tell him my decision, but I had absolutely no idea what to say. I was flooded with relief when Jonathon grabbed my hand and said, "Cathy, I don't want you to decide right now. You're obviously not ready. So, let me propose a solution. Let's stop thinking about the future, so we can enjoy our next few weeks together. I'll leave for Chicago, but then you can come and visit me during my spring vacation, after the weather warms up a bit, and I'll show you all the fun and excitement we can have together in the city. Between now and then, I'll write every week, and expect you to answer my letters. I won't give up, Cathy, but I'll give you the time to decide whether it's right for you."

Two days after Christmas, we said our good-byes. We had a wonderful dinner together and then an after-dinner walk through newly fallen snow in our Iowa County wonderland. We left each other with promises to write. I told him to mail his letters to the Logan Junction post office, since I was looking for a new room in Madison and wasn't sure where I'd be living.

And that's how we left it. I was sad to see him go, but I looked forward to a grand reunion in the spring. And I planned to write him twice a week. I wasn't about to let this wonderful man forget me.

22

LOVE LOST

Author's Note

My mother spent a day in Chicago with Carl, three years after he had left to take the job in Hammond. I used Chicago as the setting for Catherine's rendezvous with Jonathon as well. In both cases, the Chicago encounter marked an ending rather than a beginning. For quite some time, my mother was devastated that Carl was no longer in her life. She handled her grief in the same way as her fictional counterpart— by writing poetry. And like Catherine, she was eventually flattered by the attention of the university men, whom she found quite dashing.

There was some intrigue in Mother's relationship with Carl concerning a letter he had written but didn't arrive. "He mailed another letter to me after we separated, but I can't remember seeing the letter until much later," Mother recalled.

I'll expand upon Mother's doubts and suspicions and make the missing letter a crucible experience in my next book, *Strawberry Summer*.

After she moved to Madison, Mother didn't see Alice as much as she used to. Then Alice left for California to be with the man she would eventually marry. In my story, this is also what happens to Ruby.

At first when Alice left for the West, Mother thought Alice had taken her confidence and courage with her. But Mother was learning to be independent and self-sufficient. And she did a pretty good job of it, too. She purchased a used Pontiac touring car and planned a trip with her mother. They would drive across deserts and through mountains in the early 1930s at a time when few women were driving, let alone driving across lonely deserts and dangerous mountain passes. They would drive three thousand miles, two ladies alone—they were going to visit Alice.

But throughout that time, Mother would always remember Carl. She wrote, "I could never forget those deep-set blue eyes, that keen sense of humor, that calm Gary Cooper demeanor, and his singing love songs—just for me."

Jonathon and I continued to exchange letters through winter and early spring. As his spring vacation approached, I put my fears aside and looked forward to seeing him again. I even convinced myself that I'd like Chicago, but mostly I thought about how happy I would be to see Jonathon again. The day came when I got on the bus and rode to the city. And when I stepped onto the pavement, Jonathon was waiting with arms outstretched.

He tried his best to make my visit exciting and wonderful. I ate foods that I never knew existed. We rode elevators to the top of high buildings and danced all night to Sammy Kaye at the Aragon Ballroom. I loved being with Jonathon, but by the time I left, I was depressed. I knew the city wasn't right for me. Sirens kept me awake at night. Even from the top of the highest buildings, I couldn't see woodlands or fields. And the wind off Lake Michigan chilled me to the bone. When Jonathon took my arm and helped me up the steps of the departing bus, we both knew that Chicago could never be home for this little farm girl.

We continued to write for a while, but then his letters suddenly stopped. I wrote a time or two more, but never got a reply. It was a horrible feeling, going to the post office time and time again only to walk away without a cherished letter from Jonathon . This was the man who had said he didn't want to live without me, but it seemed that our week together in Chicago had sealed our fate. If he and I were not meant to be, I couldn't understand why Jonathon didn't write to tell me so. For him to abandon our grand romance without a word seemed cowardly or even cruel.

I was tempted to get on a bus to Chicago and demand that he tell me in person what he couldn't say in a letter, but my pride wouldn't let me do anything so bold. And then a terrible thought occurred to me. What if he had found someone else? Certainly there were plenty of women in

Chicago who would find the charming Jonathon Hays as irresistible as I had—and they wouldn't be yearning for the farmlands of Iowa County. I abandoned my hope of ever hearing from him again.

For a while, I was devastated. I wrote poetry to express my grief. I think that kept me sane during those days of dealing with my newfound heartache. But time passed, and I began to realize that life goes on even after a love story ends. I found solace in good books and good cinema—Jonathon had helped deepen my appreciation of both, and for that, I have been eternally grateful.

And as more time passed, I wasn't entirely bereft of male attention and companionship. I found some of the university men to be quite dashing, but in the back of my mind, I always thought that none of them could hold a candle to Jonathon.

I eventually saved enough money to afford an automobile. I was able to drive home weekends to get a good meal, wash my clothes, pick up mail, help Mother with the house cleaning, and enjoy time with Dad.

Without Jonathon to occupy my time and my heart, I needed Dad more than ever. By then, he had started his business venture with Gusta, buying Wisconsin cheese for resale in Texas. That's one thing I always remember about Gusta—she loved Wisconsin cheese. When Dad was at his lowest point, after losing the Wisconsin River farm, Gusta proposed going into the cheese business together. Dad would search for the best Wisconsin cheeses and send them to Gusta to sell to Texas oil field workers. That became a life-saving endeavor for him. And it provided time that we could be together. We went on cheese-buying trips, and I helped him package the big wheels of Swiss for shipment to Cousin Gusta.

Mother and Dad moved back to Ashley Springs when his cheese business began to prosper. With his business doing well, Dad had time to take me on outings to the trout streams around Ashley Springs. We didn't catch many fish, but our days together were glorious, full of Irish stories and laughter. We often talked about our farm near Willow, about Cousin Gusta's year there, and the people we knew. The bad memories were behind, and we thrived during our time together.

I didn't see Ruby much now that I was working in Madison. I was still getting accustomed to our new relationship. When we were together, we didn't talk about Jonathon. I suppose she decided that she'd won that battle after all.

And then, she was gone, too. Many years earlier, she had met a man who had come to our farm as a cow tester, which meant he would check our cows for butter-fat content and disease. I suppose she made a lasting impression on him. Eventually he made contact with her, and they began to write to one another. He was living in California, and she told us that she was taking the train to visit him, but we were not to worry. Two nurse friends were going with her. They returned, but she didn't. A man whom she barely knew became her husband. I was shocked at how easily Ruby had made the decision to leave her childhood home and everyone she knew behind. It was something I couldn't do, and because of that, I had lost Jonathon.

I had never loved anyone more than my sister Ruby. For most of my life, I didn't think we'd ever be apart. During my youth, I couldn't bear thinking about separation from my beloved sister. Why, I thought I'd rather have lost my left arm than lose my sister.

I felt a loss when she didn't return from California, but not like I might have a few years earlier. She had hurt me by trying so desperately to keep Jonathon and me apart. But I finally decided that it wasn't fair to blame Ruby. If Jonathon had still loved me, he would have never stopped writing. We would have found a way to be together, but I guess it was not meant to be.

Having already cried too many tears over Jonathon and adjusted to life without Ruby, I didn't expect life to deal yet another cruel blow. This one was the worst of all—a death in the family, the loss of our father, the man who was larger than life to us. Sharon, Ruby, and I—who had shared so much in life—now shared the grief of losing a parent, and our mother mourned the one true love of her life.

Dad's death came unexpectedly. His brother, Frank, had broken his ankle and needed help on his farm. Frank didn't milk cows anymore, but he did raise beef, chickens, and hogs. Dad, who never turned down someone in need, had gone over there to help.

Frank said that Dad had gone out to feed the animals, but he didn't return to the house after several hours. Frank became concerned and called his neighbor, Joe Owens. Joe found Dad slumped against the hog pen fence. He had been dead for an hour or more. The doctor said it was a massive thrombosis. We never knew why he even approached a hog pen. After his grandfather had been killed and eviscerated by hogs, Dad had vowed to never go near one again.

Mother was devastated. And I was, too. Dad was always there when we needed him.

But all of a sudden, it was over. I'd lost the only two men I had ever loved.

The shock of Dad's death was so great that I didn't dare think about it at first. I'd been so engrossed in my own topsy-turvy life that I never even considered there would come a time when he might not be with us. But after the shock wore off, that was all I could think about. We had spent our last day together tending his garden. Now I'd never tend gardens with him again.

Ruby urged our mother to move out to California with her. I thought Mother would never do it. She was too much of a Wisconsin farm girl like me, but much to my astonishment, she eventually broke down and said yes. I think Mother was afraid of what her life would be like now that Dad was gone. Perhaps being somewhere completely new and different was the only way she could cope with her loss. For me, it was another painful separation. Once again, a person I loved would be moving far away.

I promised Mother that I would drive her out to California and help get her settled, but I didn't plan on staying. I had a life to live. I'd met a new man in Madison who was handsome and a good athlete, too.

I didn't say anything to Mother about this man—not yet. I wasn't sure she'd approve as he was several years younger than me. But I planned to tell Ruby about him—above all that he looked just like Jonathon.

THERE'LL BE MORE

The next book, *Strawberry Summer,* tells the story of seventy-five-year-old Catherine left with choices. What will it be—a man, her son, or a life of independence?

⸺ ABOUT THE AUTHOR ⸺

Harold William Thorpe grew up in Southwest Wisconsin and lived on farms for brief periods when he was very young. He spent many happy hours at his relative's farms, and during his teen years he detasseled corn, worked two summers as a live-in farm laborer, worked one summer as a Surge milking machine sales and service man, and worked part of another summer as a United States Department of Agriculture field man.

After high school, he graduated from UW-Platteville with an education degree. He worked for eleven years in Janesville, Wisconsin — first as a general education and special education teacher, then the last four years as a school psychologist. During these years he started a business and earned a masters degree in educational psychology at UW-Madison. Afterward, he left Janesville for Utah State University where he earned a doctorate degree in education.

Upon returning to Wisconsin he took a position at UW-Oshkosh where he initiated a program to prepare students to teach the learning disabled. For the next twenty-five years he taught classes, supervised student teachers and graduate students, and served in administrative positions as a graduate program coordinator, a department chairperson, and a college associate dean. But his first love was conducting research that produced more than twenty-five publications in education and psychology journals.

After retirement, he decided to learn how to write fiction. *Puppet on a String is Book III of the O'Shaughnessy Chronicles.*